Be Still, My Soul

MYSTERIES OF THE WEST #1

FAITH BLUM

Wild Blue Wonder PRESS

Cover design and interior formatting: Hannah Linder Designs |
https://hannahlinderdesigns.com/
Formatting: Faith Blum | www.faithblum.com
Copy editor: Andrea Renee Cox |
https://andreareneecox.com/editing-services/
Proofreader: Kelsey Bryant |
https://kelseybryantauthor.weebly.com/editing.html

Be Still, My Soul is a work of fiction. Though this book is based on historical
facts, all characterizations and descriptions of people, names, places, and
things are from the author's imagination. Any similarities to real people,
living or dead, are entirely coincidental.

All Scriptures are quoted from the King James Version as found on
www.biblegateway.com unless otherwise noted.

Other Titles by Faith Blum

Contents

To Joanne Bischof
Your encouragement and advice kept me going when I was
plotting this book. Thank you for all your help.

Be still, my soul: the Lord is on thy side.
Bear patiently the cross of grief or pain.
Leave to thy God to order and provide;
In every change, He faithful will remain.
Be still, my soul: thy best, thy heav'nly Friend
Through thorny ways leads to a joyful end.

Be still, my soul: thy God doth undertake
To guide the future, as He has the past.
Thy hope, thy confidence let nothing shake;
All now mysterious shall be bright at last.
Be still, my soul: the waves and winds still know
His voice Who ruled them while He dwelt below.

Be still, my soul: when dearest friends depart,
And all is darkened in the vale of tears,
Then shalt thou better know His love, His heart,
Who comes to soothe thy sorrow and thy fears.
Be still, my soul: thy Jesus can repay
From His own fullness all He takes away.

Be still, my soul: the hour is hast'ning on
When we shall be forever with the Lord.
When disappointment, grief, and fear are gone,
Sorrow forgot, love's purest joys restored.
Be still, my soul: when change and tears are past
All safe and blessed we shall meet at last.

Be still, my soul: begin the song of praise
On earth, believing, to Thy Lord on high;
Acknowledge Him in all thy words and ways,
So shall He view thee with a well-pleased eye.
Be still, my soul: the Sun of life divine
Through passing clouds shall but more brightly shine.

"Let him that stole steal no more: but rather let him labour, working with his hands the thing which is good, that he may have to give to him that needeth."
– Ephesians 4:28

Prologue

Near Angleton, Texas
1865

Trying to live in two worlds was near impossible. But his growing-up years left Carsten Whitford accustomed to that kind of life. With his pa, Carsten lived for the thrill and danger of robbery. His pa never got caught while Carsten helped him, and Carsten took pride in it.

Then there was Ma. With her, Carsten was the dutiful son, trying his hardest to pretend he believed everything she wanted him to about God and His love.

As he lived his two lives, Carsten always feared those worlds would prove impossible to mix in the end.

The War Between the States had finally ended a couple months earlier. Pa hadn't fought in the war. He didn't think either side was worth dying for. Whenever someone came, he disappeared for a few days so he couldn't get drafted by force.

Carsten was one of the lucky ones, being able to have his pa home. His three friends' fathers all fought for the Confederacy. Those that came back alive had a different outlook on life after the bloody war. Although he had his pa, if Carsten was honest with himself, maybe it would have been better if his pa had fought in the war and stopped teaching him how to be a thief. After all, Pa's main income during the lean years on the farm was stealing.

From the time he turned seven, Carsten had helped his pa get into houses and take the residents' valuables. Pa would take them to another town to sell and get their supplies. It was their secret and years before Ma knew what they did together. Carsten was going into other people's houses and trying not to get caught.

When he was ten, he heard a sermon about stealing being wrong. Carsten thought about telling Ma but decided Pa must know what he was doing. He wouldn't tell his own son to do something that was a sin.

Now, at thirteen, the thrill he got from helping Pa had worn off some. The pleasure had to be better if he did some thievery all by himself—and then he could prove to Pa that he was just like him. Carsten's goal wasn't making a lot of money, so he stole little trinkets that were unlikely to be missed and showed them to Pa. And he was right. The delight definitely heightened when he stole by himself.

Then came the fateful day he went into the house of a girl from church. Luella Comstock. She was the same age as Carsten, almost to the day, and much better at schoolwork than he was. He envied that about her. She seemed to do sums and reading so effortlessly.

It was dusk, and the time most people ate dinner, usually a good time to do some petty thievery. He sneaked in through a window at the back and made his way through the house and up the stairs. There were no lamps lit up there, so he went into one of the rooms and saw a dresser with jewelry scattered on top. He grabbed a piece and made it to the door before a voice arrested his movements.

"What are you doing?" It was Luella.

Carsten's heart stopped. "Um. Nothing." He turned, hiding his hands behind his back.

Luella was on the bed, her blonde hair shining in the dimming light from the window. "Why are you in Mother's room?"

"I…" He ducked his head. "I was going to steal this." He held up the necklace.

"Why?"

"Do I need a reason?"

Luella nodded.

Carsten sighed. "Oh. I did it because it's fun."

Luella stood, crossing her arms over her chest and glaring at him. "Fun? To take the lone pearl necklace Mother has? That Papa worked hard to be able to buy?"

A strange pain pricked at his heart. "When you put it that way, it doesn't sound very fun. I'm sorry." He took two large strides to the dresser and set the necklace down.

Luella smiled. "Thank you."

"Luella?" A man's voice floated down the hall.

"Yes, Papa?"

"Dinner is ready."

Luella gazed at him, and Carsten wondered what she was thinking. Would she let him go, or would he have to face her pa? "Papa, come here, please. I'm in Mother's room."

Carsten steeled himself for the wrath of whatever Mr. Comstock would do.

Mr. Comstock entered the room, and his piercing blue eyes rested on him and narrowed. "What is a young man doing in here?"

Carsten glanced from father to daughter and back again. Luella didn't talk, so Carsten gulped and opened his mouth, but nothing came out.

"Well? Who are you, boy?" Mr. Comstock raised an eyebrow.

"I'm Carsten."

"What are you doing here?"

Did he dare lie? Something Ma said made him stop and tell the truth. "I was going to steal something, but your daughter caught me, so I returned it."

Mr. Comstock stroked his short, medium-brown beard. "I like an honest man. You go to church, don't you?"

"Yes, sir."

"Hm. Let's go down to the marshal's office and see what we can work out."

Carsten chose not to look at Luella. Pretty as she was, she had turned him in.

Mr. Comstock let him walk without restraints past the Feed and Seed Store, the café, the hotel, and the post office before crossing the street to get to the marshal's office.

Marshal Daniel Lydick stood as they entered. "What can I do for you two?"

Mr. Comstock put a hand on Carsten's arm. "We need to discuss an appropriate punishment for this young man. He got caught trying to take something from our home. He chose to put it back when my daughter caught him, so I'm inclined to be lenient, though I think he should face some consequences for his actions."

Marshal Lydick shook his head. "He should. Hmmm. What about community service?"

"Yes, that would be acceptable."

Would Carsten get a say in this? Did it matter if he did?

"We have some dust buildup in this office and at the church," the marshal said. "I think that would work. What do you think, boy?"

Carsten straightened. "My name's Carsten. Thank you, sir, for not putting me in jail."

Marshal Lydick chuckled. "You may go home now. But don't do any more stealing, or I will put you in jail."

"Yes, sir." Carsten hightailed it out of there. He needed to get home. Ma would worry if he didn't. He needed to talk to her. How was he going to stop when the pull was so strong? How was he going to tell Pa he got caught?

He stopped in the middle of the road right outside of town when he thought of Pa. He'd be upset and disappointed. Carsten's backside burned as he thought about the tanning Pa might give him. He started walking again, slower this time. Every dark shape of a tree made him jump. Not that there were many, but there were enough.

CHAPTER 1

Change

Early March 1870

One beautiful spring day, Carsten headed to town. Ma needed a few supplies from the General Store, and he needed to see if his seeds were in. Ever since Pa went to jail for armed robbery four years earlier, Carsten was the man of the house and in charge of the farm and all the planting, growing, harvesting, and selling of alfalfa to the nearby ranchers. No sisters or brothers. Just his ma and him.

For once in the last week, he didn't need to work the fields, and a gentle saunter seemed more fitting somehow. As he walked, it occurred to him that it had been almost five years to the day since he stopped stealing.

He passed the big magnolia tree and stopped in its shade for a few minutes. He had never whiffed anything similar to it. He made his feet go one in front of the other toward town. If he didn't, he wouldn't make it home in time for lunch. And Ma's lunches were not to be missed! None of her meals were, come to think of it.

The closer he got, the more houses there were. He strode

into town, acting more confident than he felt. Ever since Pa's arrest, the revelation of his part in the previous robberies, and his own petty thievery, Carsten had become an outcast. A bad seed. No matter what he did, very few people wanted to be near him.

Carsten started at the General Store. He found everything on Ma's list and brought it all to the counter.

"Ya want this on credit?" Mr. Martin asked.

Carsten shook his head. "I'll pay for it."

Mr. Martin added the totals and wrapped it all in brown paper, then tied it with string. "Here ya go."

Carsten paid him, took his packages, and walked past two ladies. They stopped talking as he went by. At the door, he glanced over his shoulder and saw them whispering to each other, giving him side glances. He sighed as he stepped out into the fresh air.

"There you are." A feminine voice spoke near him.

Carsten jerked his head in her direction and saw blonde curls escaping her bun as always. "Luella. How are you?"

"I saw you walking into town but then lost you. I'm doin' well, thank you. Do you have more shoppin' to do?"

"A little. I need to order somethin' at the print shop. It's a surprise for Ma. And I need to check on my seed order."

"Excitin'. Can I ask what you're ordering for your ma?"

Carsten bit back a smile. "You can ask. Doesn't mean I'll tell." He winked at her.

Luella giggled. It wasn't as annoying as some women's. It was cute. But he wasn't about to tell her that. She was eighteen and a grown woman and didn't want to be cute. At least that's what Ma always said.

"What are you gettin' her?"

Carsten took a deep breath. "She's always wanted more things to hang on our parlor wall, so I'm gonna get a Scripture verse printed out. Then all I need to do is figure out how to make a picture frame for it."

"She'll love that. What verse are you doin'?"

"Maybe you can help me pick. Her favorite verse is the first bit of Psalm 46:10: 'Be still, and know that I am God.' But she also likes the last part of Joshua 24:15: 'As for me and my house, we will serve the Lord.' I don't know which she'd want the most."

Luella's nose wrinkled. "That's hard. They're both such good verses. Can you do both?"

He grimaced. "No. I shouldn't even be doin' one. The alfalfa crop isn't doing as well as I needed it to this year."

Luella put a hand on his arm. "I'm sorry. You should do her favorite verse, then. Maybe in a couple years, you can do the other one."

Carsten grinned. "Thank you, Luella. I appreciate your help." He looked up at the sky. "I should finish my errands here and hurry home. It was nice chattin' with you." Something flashed in the sun in his periphery, and he searched for it. The marshal's badge. He was across the street, staring at Luella and him. What did he want? Carsten hadn't done anything wrong. Not since that day five years earlier, when Luella caught him. Well, and the other time no one knew about. The marshal had been different the last couple years. He'd always been gruff but at least kind. But ever since Pa was sent to prison, Marshal Lydick had been harder on anyone who was even remotely doing bad.

"Are you all right?"

Carsten shook the thoughts away and brought his attention back to Luella. "I'm fine. Got lost in thought for a second."

Luella searched his face. "If you're sure."

"I'm sure."

"Well, goodbye, then. And good luck figurin' out exactly what to do for your ma."

"Thank you." He walked down the boardwalk and tried not to look across the street to see if Marshal Lydick was still there. It didn't matter. Carsten hadn't done anything wrong. The marshal was just doing his job. But hadn't Carsten proven he had changed? Apparently not enough, since people still talked about him behind his back and the marshal watched him intently.

Carsten sighed as he stepped into the print shop. The owner, Luis Graves, stood behind the counter.

"Good day, young man. How can I help you?"

"I would like a print made for my ma but want to see some designs first."

"Of course. Carey, bring our samples in here, please."

A young man with unruly brown hair came in from the back room. "Here you go, Mr. Graves." He saw Carsten and scowled before whispering something to Mr. Graves.

"Nonsense," Mr. Graves stated. "I'm sure there's nothing to worry about. Now, let's see here. What kind of print are you looking for?"

Carsten resisted the urge to flee Carey Eldridge's stare. "A Bible verse. Psalm 46:10: 'Be still, and know that I am God.' Something big enough to see from across a small room."

"Would something like this work?" Mr. Graves showed him five samples, and Carsten examined each one. He had a hard time imagining what the verse would look like, so he finally chose a design he thought his ma would like most.

"Do I pay you now or when I pick it up?"

"Later is fine," Mr. Graves replied. "It should be finished in a little over a week."

"Thank you, Mr. Graves. I'll come back then."

Mr. Graves waved as Carsten turned and stepped outside. The sun had already made it to the peak of the sky. He was late.

He stopped quickly in to see about his seed and was told it would be another week. The trek home went faster than going to town. He was hungry and knew Ma would be waiting.

"I'm home, Ma," he said as he burst through the door.

"I was beginning to wonder."

"Sorry. Things took longer than I thought, and I... I talked a bit to Luella."

Ma smiled. "How's she doin'?"

"She's doin' well." He put the packages on the table. "Here are your items. Do you want help putting them away?"

Ma patted his back. "No. They can wait until after we eat. I know you're probably starving."

Carsten grinned. "Not quite starving."

Ma laughed. "I'm sure. Let's eat."

"Thanks, Ma. You're the best."

Carsten sat at the head of the table. It seemed so big with only two people around it, but someday, he would have a wife and kids of his own sitting here. He said a short blessing over the food and dished some stew onto his plate.

"What did you and Luella talk about?" Ma asked as Carsten put his first bite in his mouth.

He swallowed a bit too soon and tried not to choke on the large piece of carrot. "Mostly small talk. Then I had to finish up so I wasn't too late for lunch."

"What did you need her advice on?"

"Hm?" He pretended to act dumb. "Ma, this stew is amazing. What did you do different?"

"Nuh-uh. You're not gettin' away with ignoring my question."

"A surprise," he answered.

"Very well. I'll drop the matter for now. As for the stew, there is nothing different about it."

"Maybe I'm hungrier than normal or somethin'."

"Or you were tryin' to get out of answering my question and had to think of somethin' quick."

Carsten shrugged and kept eating. He finished the bowl of stew and stood up. "I'll be out in the fields, if you need anything."

Ma put a hand on his. "I love you, son."

"I love you, too, Ma."

CARSTEN FINISHED up what he could that day a couple hours before dinner, so he asked if he could go find his friends at the lake. At eighteen, he didn't have to ask, but he liked to get Ma's permission anyway.

"Of course. Be home before dark."

"Yes, Ma."

He hurried to the Bar X Ranch. Amos Raskins was outside his pa's house with Edmund Flinn as Carsten rushed up the lane in their direction. "Hiya, Amos and Edmund!"

"Carsten!" Edmund shouted. "We were comin' your way. Kit can't come today. His pa needed help gettin' the calves ready for branding."

"Is it that season already?" Carsten asked.

Amos rubbed the back of his neck. "Gettin' there. I can't believe it either. Seems like yesterday since last year's calves were branded. Now we've got yearlings who are gonna be mamas soon."

Carsten finally reached them. "Are you two free for the rest of the afternoon?"

"Yep."

"Swimmin' or fishin'?" Edmund asked.

"Swimmin'," Amos answered. "The fish won't be biting this time of day anyway."

The three young men raced for the lake. Edmund reached it first as always. He had the longest legs of the group. Carsten swam and splashed and dunked with Amos and Edmund for a couple hours. By then, they were tuckered out and ready to slow down. They floated on their backs for a bit and finally got out of the water to dry off. In the warmth of the sun, it didn't take long.

"How is the alfalfa this year?" Edmund asked.

"It's growing. I don't know how well, though. I'm afraid it's gonna be a sparser crop than the last one."

"Isn't the first crop usually your best?" Amos questioned.

"Yeah." Carsten tried not to sound desperate. "It's okay. I'll make it work somehow. I always do."

Amos sighed. "Sure, but you shouldn't have to do it all on your own. Isn't there some way we can help?"

"No," Carsten said. "Unless you know a way to make it grow better and thicker that doesn't cost money."

"You know of a way that *does* cost money?" Edmund asked.

"I don't know. It's a rumor I heard."

Edmund chuckled. "Rumors are pretty unreliable. Remember the one about old Mrs. Higgins?"

Amos and Carsten joined his laughter.

"Yeah," Amos said. "They said she had twenty kids, and some people actually believed it. Then she straightened everyone out by sayin' she had four. How do people get things so wrong?"

"Because they listen to other people," Edmund answered, "instead of going to the source. All people had to do was go up to Mrs. Higgins and ask, and she would've gladly told them about each of her kids."

If that was true, why didn't people come to Carsten and ask if he was still a thief instead of assuming he was going to mess up? Hadn't he changed enough for them to know he wasn't that type of person?

"What's eating you, Carsten?" Amos asked.

Carsten startled. "Huh? Oh. Nothin'. I should get home. I have a couple things to do before Ma has supper ready. Thanks for swimmin' with me."

Amos narrowed his eyes. "Sure. Always happy to. Though, with brandin' coming, I'm not sure we'll be able to do it much for a while."

Carsten tapped his foot. "Good to know. Thanks for informing me. If you see Kit before I do, tell him we missed his antics today."

Amos and Edmund laughed and waved.

Carsten strolled home. He wasn't in a huge hurry, but he didn't want to answer their questions. He couldn't answer them. Amos and Edmund were sons of prosperous ranchers.

Especially Amos. His grandfather established Bar X in the thirties. It had been the most successful ranch in the county for decades.

Neither of the young men were sons of a struggling farmer who took to stealing if he didn't have enough money. They couldn't understand what Carsten went through after having a father put in jail or having public sins of his own.

Of course, then there was the palomino and his owner. He shook his head. No, he had to stay away from those types of thoughts. That was in the past. What had happened had happened, and he needed to be done with the guilt.

He meandered home along the rocky road lined with ankle-high grass and budding flowers. Taking the long way wasn't smart since he had things he had to do before supper, but the time to clear his head would be valuable. He'd had such a good day until he let his own thoughts intrude on his happiness. Why did he sabotage himself? Why couldn't he have had a normal life? One without a history of criminals.

Their small, simple farmhouse loomed on the horizon. Well, *loomed* made it seem bigger than it actually was. Their house was a simple log cabin with one window on each of its four sides. In front, they had a simple wooden door with a leather hook and latch for a handle, front and back.

Small but cozy. And his home. He'd been born in that house and lived there his whole life. Despite some of the bad memories, he wanted to live there the rest of his life. Eventually, he wanted to be buried out back in the place Pa and Ma had chosen for themselves.

For now, he needed to get the last of his work for the day done and get himself washed up for supper.

CHAPTER 2
Accused

Carsten and his ma sat at the table eating her tasty biscuits and beans without speaking. Although common foods for ranchers on the trail, Carsten doubted theirs tasted so good. He ended up with seconds and thirds of the beans plus four biscuits. After all, he was a growing boy.

"How are Edmund, Kit, and Amos?" Ma asked.

"Edmund and Amos are well. Kit couldn't join us today. He had to help his pa with branding. Edmund, Amos, and I had a good time cooling off in the lake and chatting some afterward."

"You have such good friends."

"You say that every time I get together with them."

Ma smiled. "I know. Can't I be glad about something many times over?"

"I suppose." He chewed his lip. "Do you have friends?"

"Not really."

"Why not?"

Ma set her fork down and stared off into the distance. "I'm the wife of an armed robber and had no clue what was going on. The few friends I had before your father's arrest have abandoned me."

Carsten hung his head. "I'm sorry. I should've told you about Pa sooner. And tried to stop sooner myself."

"It's not your fault. It's Foster's fault. Him and his criminal-minded family. I don't blame you. You were a child doing what your father told you to. You didn't know it was wrong. And even after you realized it was, you looked up to him as you should have been able to."

"Did you know about Pa's father and grandfather when you married him?"

Ma finished chewing her bite of biscuit. "You mean their criminal activities? I knew they'd both spent time in jail but didn't know the extent."

"If you had, would you still have married Pa?"

Ma took a deep breath and looked up at him with her big brown eyes. "I don't know. I really don't."

Carsten moved the last forkful of beans around on his plate. "I'm glad you did, or I wouldn't be here."

Ma laughed. "So am I, Carsten." She let out a long breath. "We should clean up the food."

The door burst open as she stood. Ma screamed, and Carsten jumped up and moved between Ma and the intruder.

"Who are..." The words stopped in his mouth as the town marshal came into view. Alone. "What is going on?"

"You need to come with me, Carsten."

"Why?"

Marshal Lydick pulled out the handcuffs. "You ought to know why. You stole a few things today."

"That's not possible," Carsten said.

Ma came closer and put a hand on his arm as he spoke.

"I was in town for a short time, and unless Luella had something to do with it, I couldn't have done anything."

"What about at the print shop?"

Carsten swallowed hard. Not from guilt, of course, but he didn't want Ma to know. "I ordered something. That's all."

"You didn't take anything?"

"No! I don't steal anymore."

Marshal Lydick narrowed his eyes. "All the evidence points to you, so I'm going to have to take you in, at least overnight, until we can clear this up at the trial."

"No!" Ma exclaimed. "He didn't do it. You can't take him."

"Before I go, search for the stolen items," Carsten said. "I'll consent to a search as long as you don't break anything."

Marshal Lydick scowled. "You've had plenty of time to hide it."

"I've been busy all day. And there aren't many places on this property to hide things."

The marshal grumbled but did as Carsten asked and searched everywhere.

While he did, Carsten took his ma aside. "He's gonna take me in regardless. Please don't worry about me. I'll be fine. But in the morning, you should go to the Bar X and talk to Mr. Raskins. He'll be able to help you and should have ideas on helping me. And you can ask Amos to keep an eye on the crops if I can't get out in a couple days."

Ma held his face in her hands. Under normal circumstances, he hated when she did that, but today, he was more than willing to allow it. "I will pray for you," she said. "We will get through this."

He tried to smile, but it wouldn't come. Instead, he hugged Ma tight until he saw Marshal Lydick approaching.

"Nothin' in the house, and it better not be in the barn."

"What am I supposed to have stolen?"

"I won't reveal that to the thief." He pulled out the handcuffs again and took a step closer. "We're going to the jail, where you will spend some time while I investigate."

Tears streamed down Ma's face. "Please don't do this."

"I have to, Mrs. Whitford."

Ma sank onto a nearby chair and bowed her head.

"I'll make this right, Ma. I'll be out soon." Carsten jerked against the marshal pulling him out the door. "They can't have anything concrete on me. I didn't do this."

"Shut up," Marshal Lydick growled. "Come on. We have to get to town."

"Ma, I'll be fine. Don't worry about me." Carsten glanced behind them as they reached the door.

Ma still sat at the table, her head bowed. Her mouth moved almost imperceptibly, and Carsten knew she was praying. Just one more hug. He needed her arms around him one more time, but the marshal pulled him in the opposite direction.

What was going on? Why was this happening? Who had accused him of stealing?

The marshal stopped near one of the two horses out front. He helped Carsten mount a horse and tied his handcuffed hands to the pommel of the saddle. The marshal then took the reins in his hands and mounted his own horse, holding Carsten's reins as a lead rope.

The whole, slow ride to town, Carsten fumed. How could this be happening? He had never been outright accused of something he didn't do. He hadn't taken anything from either shop he'd been in. Not a tiny corner of paper, not even a written quote as to how much his wall hanging would cost. Stealing wasn't something he would do anymore. It wasn't even his style of robbery. If he were to steal something—not that he would now, but *if*—it would be at dusk, not morning. And it would be in a house, not a shop.

The marshal seemed intent on not listening to him, though. Ever since the day his father had been arrested and it was learned that Pa had been stealing for years right under the marshal's nose, Marshal Lydick hadn't been the same. He'd become broody and discontent. Carsten didn't know who else had seen this in the marshal, but apparently, now that someone else was stealing, it was Carsten's turn to be accused. It made sense, in a way, for the marshal to go after the only other person in town who'd stolen before, but Carsten had changed, too, but for the better. Did no one see that?

So here they were. Riding into town very uncomfortably. He'd heard of criminals getting tied to a saddle like this but never thought about how much it would hurt one's back. Carsten was thankful it was a quiet time of evening in this part of town as people ate their own dinners. There would be few, if anyone, to see him riding in resembling a criminal. He had enough problems with people thinking of him as a lawless man without them seeing this.

Marshal Lydick tugged Carsten off the horse, took him inside, and shoved him into a jail cell. Once he locked him inside, the marshal said, "Put your hands through the bars, and I'll take the cuffs off."

Carsten did as he said.

"I need to go make my rounds, but I'll be back, so don't think of trying anything."

"Like what? I'm innocent, so it's best to stay put until you realize that. Or prove it."

The marshal narrowed his eyes and shook his head as he left.

Carsten was alone. In a jail cell. No one to talk to. No one to distract him from thinking too much. There wasn't even a drunk in the cell next to him.

He lay down and stared at the filthy ceiling above him. A musty, sweaty odor surrounded him, and he gagged. Did he want to know if the blankets had been washed recently? Probably not.

Maybe this was God's way of punishing him for the horse four years earlier. He'd known then it was wrong to take it for a ride.

Carsten had always loved palomino horses. Their light-brown coats and cream manes and tails were so handsome. Sure, they looked dirty faster than other horses, but what did that matter? Horses needed to be groomed often anyway.

One day when he was fourteen, Carsten wandered home from Kit's and saw the horse ground tied near a small camp. No one was around, so Carsten gave in to temptation and took a short ride on the beautiful mare.

A few days later, when he was in town, he heard someone say that the owner of a palomino mare had died. Since then, it had torn him up to think it might have been his fault. Had the owner returned to his camp and found his horse gone and died from shock? Or died from lack of water because he didn't have a horse to ride to the nearest river? Carsten couldn't know and never would.

He sat up and rubbed his temples. The stone walls in this cell combined with the air cooling down outside made the skin on his arms prickle, but he actually didn't mind. He liked to think the cold helped his guilt, but it didn't really.

He stood and paced the small room. It was six strides by six strides. At least for Carsten. Back and forth, around in a square, diagonal in an X. He did them all.

Was this how a caged animal felt? No animal should be caged. They were innocent of anything and yet people put them in enclosed spaces so they could go look at them.

Carsten tried to take a deep breath but couldn't. His lungs only let him take short, shallow breaths. He clenched his fists. For the first time, he wanted to punch something. But there wasn't anything safe here to punch without hurting himself.

He yelled in frustration, picked up the cot, and threw it against the wall as hard as he could. He closed his eyes and concentrated on expanding his chest and forcing himself to take deep breaths. This wasn't like him. He didn't get angry. He didn't take anger out on objects or people.

After a minute of deep breathing, he opened his eyes and unclenched his fists. The cot was a sturdy piece of work and had survived his abuse. The thin mat and even thinner blanket were both on the grimy floor. He sighed. As Ma always said, there were consequences to your actions.

Carsten picked up the cot and put the thin mattress on, then sat. He had to adjust his thinking. Do something to get his mind off where he was. His arrest.

Someone had taken something from the print shop. It hadn't been him, but many people in town apparently didn't believe that. So what did the mystery thief take, and who else could have been there around the time Carsten had?

If he could get out of here, he would investigate. From what the marshal had said, it didn't sound like he would even try to prove Carsten innocent. He thought of asking his friends to help but decided against it. He couldn't drag them into this. He had to do it on his own.

The only easy, and logical, item to steal from the print shop was paper. But why steal paper? And how would you hide it from them and the others walking through town? 'Course, you'd only have to hide it while in the store. The first question still applied, though. Why steal paper? It wasn't all that expensive, and anyone who used a lot of it would be able to afford it. Unless a kid needed some for school and was too poor to pay for it. But then, why go to the print shop when the General Store would be easier to steal from? Would the marshal lie about the place?

Carsten sighed. Was there something else in the print shop he missed when he was in there? Did they have special pens? Who knew? Not him. Maybe it was one of the samples that got stolen. He hadn't accidentally grabbed one and kept it with him, had he? No. Ma would've noticed—and the marshal would have found it. And all Carsten had put on the table when he got home were the brown paper packages he'd gotten for her.

Well, maybe he would have to enlist his friends to help him after all. As he thought about it, a knot formed in his stomach. He couldn't endanger them, but it was more than that. Last time he'd asked someone for help, it ended with him stuck in the mud without anybody to help him. Besides the man running away after allowing him to fall there in the first place. His friends were great and all, and he definitely trusted them, but not as much as he knew he should.

He needed to change that but didn't know how. He also needed to figure out why he didn't trust them. Or maybe he just needed to figure out something. Anything.

He stood and paced the cell again but stopped as a thought popped into his head. He hadn't prayed in over a year. How could he forget such a simple thing? He was a Christian and should be talking to God daily. Guilt gnawed at him. He hadn't prayed or read the Bible for at least a year.

He needed to get back into the habit of reading the Bible, but that wasn't going to happen until he got out of jail. In the meantime, he could try his hand at praying again.

"Hi, God. It's me. I haven't talked to You in a while. And now that I am, I don't know what to say. I'm in a bit of trouble right now, as I'm sure You know. I didn't do what they say I did. But I don't know how to convince them of that. Maybe You can help with that. Want to put some of the evidence out there for them to find?"

A forced laugh left his mouth. Like anyone would even see the evidence for him. "If that's possible, anyway. I don't know what else to do here. How can I prove to people that I'm different from when I was stealing things? Or is that something I'm supposed to leave up to You, and that's why it hasn't been working recently?"

Carsten sighed. It had been a long day, and he needed to try to sleep. He moved the blanket and lay down. As he pulled the coarse covering over him, he breathed another short prayer. "God, help me get some sleep tonight. Despite everything that happened today. Thanks."

CHAPTER 3
Obadiah

A blinding light jerked him out of a deep sleep. Carsten sat up, and the light left his eyes. Sun shone through the bars above him and hit the cot right where his head had been. Apparently, this cell had its own little alarm on sunny days. He stretched and yawned. He preferred Ma's way to wake him: the smell of coffee brewing and the sound of bacon sizzling.

He hopped off the cot and did a quick pace around the cell to try to warm up his limbs. When they were warmer, he sat back down and waited. For what, he didn't know. What could he wait for? He had nothing to do in here. The least they could do was provide books. 'Course, would that even help some people? Probably not. Half the people who ended up in here were likely illiterate.

He sighed. It would be a long day if there was nothing to do. Would the marshal even come back to see if Carsten survived the night? If the marshal did return, would he bring food, and if so, how bad would it be? Surely they had to feed prisoners.

Carsten stood and patrolled the cell again. It was too small for the pacing to be satisfying, but at least it got him moving.

He needed movement or he would go crazy. Striding around the cell might not be enough either. It was too soon to tell.

"Carsten!" a voice shouted. "Stop walking around in there!"

Must be the marshal. He could hear him pacing? "If I don't?"

"I'll come in and make you stop."

That didn't sound pleasant. Carsten sat on the cot. "Am I going to get breakfast sometime this morning?"

"Depends on if there's enough when Marcia comes by."

"Who's Marcia?"

"My lady friend."

Carsten shook his head. Marcia was the marshal's lady friend? Ironic. And Carsten doubted she would bring any extra food. Unless Marcia knew he was here and took pity on him. So what could he think about to get his mind off his already grumbly stomach? Maybe he could think about how Marcia could stand being around the marshal for any length of time.

The opening of a door interrupted his thoughts. "Mornin', Marshal," a deep voice said. Obadiah. Amos's father. The man who'd taken Carsten under his wing after Pa went to prison.

"What can I do for you, Mr. Raskins?" The question came with the scraping of a chair.

"I need to talk to Carsten."

"We don't allow visitors for prisoners."

"You let Carsten visit his pa when Foster was here."

Carsten could almost hear the scowl on Marshal Lydick's face.

"Fine. But only for a few minutes."

"Thank you."

Keys rattled in the door between the office and the cells.

Obadiah came toward Carsten and stopped right in front of the bars. "Did you do it?"

25

His question stung. Did he think Carsten did it? How could he? Carsten took a deep breath and looked Obadiah in the eyes. "No."

Obadiah gave a curt nod. "I didn't think so. I'm gonna try to get you out of here. I can't make any guarantees, but I'll do my best. Do you know of anything that I can tell him?"

"I don't even know what got stolen. All I can tell you is that Ma saw everythin' I took home."

"Hm. That might not be enough for the marshal."

"I know. But it might be something. He also searched my house and found nothin'." Carsten sighed. "Thank you for anything you can do."

Obadiah turned and strode out to the office. "I want him released until the trial."

"No."

"I'll pay you some money. You have to give it back after the trial. If he doesn't show up at the trial, the money remains yours."

There was a pause. "No."

"Why not? He didn't steal anything. You searched his house. Did you find something?"

"No, but he might have hidden it somewhere else."

Obadiah growled. "I can guarantee he won't steal anything while he is out. All you need to do is look into this matter and find the real thief. I'll make sure Carsten doesn't do anything in the meantime."

"How?"

This time, the pause was on Obadiah's side. "I'll check in on him every night I can and talk to his mother about making sure she is with him whenever she can. I can also send my son to stay with Carsten until the trial if you need more assurance."

"Amos and Carsten are friends. How do I know Amos isn't a thief, too?"

Obadiah growled again. "My son is not a thief and never will be. Why would he need to steal anything?"

"Why would Carsten?"

"Carsten's father was a bad influence on him," Obadiah said. "Amos had me as a good influence and is the son of a wealthy rancher. You've been keeping an eye on Carsten, haven't you?"

"Yes."

"Has he done anything illegal in the last five years?"

"Not that I know of. But this last theft happened in a store. I can't follow him into every store he enters."

Obadiah's spurs jangled when he stomped a foot. "Did he know you were watching him?"

"He saw me watching, so probably."

"Why would he steal something when he knew you were there?"

The marshal didn't say anything for a while. "Fine. I'll let you take him home. But if he does anything..."

"I know," Obadiah said. "Thank you."

There was silence again as Carsten stood and waited for them to let him out. When they didn't come for a while, he almost sat but didn't. They would be here soon. They had to. Obadiah was probably figuring out how much to give the marshal. Something Carsten would have to figure out how to pay back without offending Obadiah. And without ruining himself.

A couple minutes later, keys jangled nearby, and Carsten jerked his head up to see Marshal Lydick heading his way. The scowl on his face showed what he thought of this whole situation.

"Go," he said as he swung the door open. "Before I change my mind."

"Thank you," Carsten said and darted past him and into the office, where Obadiah waited. "Let's get out of here."

Obadiah trailed behind him. Once they were outside, Obadiah stopped. "Why are you in such a hurry?"

"I want to get home. To Ma."

"Okay, but first, I want to talk with you. Are you hungry?"

Carsten turned to him. "Starved."

"Let's go to the café and eat there. While we eat, we can talk."

"I don't want to be owin' you a lot of money," Carsten said. "What you paid the marshal and now the café."

Obadiah shook his head. "You don't owe me anythin'. I enjoy treating my friends to good things once in a while." He put an arm around Carsten's shoulders. "Let's go."

Carsten went with him. Not that he had a choice, but he didn't mind. He liked the café's food almost as much as he liked his ma's.

Once they sat and had their orders in, Carsten waited for Obadiah to talk. Carsten had no idea what the man wanted to talk about and was kind of scared. Obadiah wasn't a cruel man, but he was tough. And Carsten liked that. Pa had been a bit too lenient, which he had learned from his pa. Carsten wanted to be more like Obadiah than Pa. For various reasons. One big one being that Obadiah was a Christian and upstanding citizen.

Obadiah cleared his throat. "What are you going to do now that you are free for a time?"

"Find a way to prove my innocence," Carsten answered immediately. "I didn't do this. The marshal already searched my house, so I'm not sure how, but I'll do anything I need to as long as it's legal. I'm not going to jail for somethin' I didn't do."

"How are you going to investigate without offending the marshal?"

"I don't know."

Obadiah smiled, a contemplative look showing up within seconds. "I think it's a good idea for you to investigate, if you decide to. I don't think the marshal has any plans to look into anyone else who might have stolen whatever it was."

"He didn't tell you either?"

"No. I didn't come right out and ask, though. That's the first thing you need to find out."

Their food arrived, and Obadiah prayed for it. They both ate a good portion before talking again.

"Are you still drawn to stealing?" Obadiah asked.

Carsten swallowed his bite of pancake a little early and coughed. "A little. But I don't do it. And I won't. I know it's not right."

"I'm glad you're honest about it. What do you think you can do about the temptation?"

Carsten startled. He hadn't thought about that. All he'd done was try to ignore the temptation and stay out of town when the pull came. What else could he do? "Not go to town when I'm weak and could be tempted."

"What if you don't think you will be tempted and then come to town and you are?"

Carsten's fork hovered midair. "I don't know. I guess I'll not do anything. Or"—he set his fork down—"stop comin' to town."

"You can't stop coming to town to avoid possible temptations."

Carsten sighed. "I know. I need to figure something else out. Looking into who stole from the print shop could satisfy my thrill for excitement."

"That would be a valid option."

"I'll also make sure I do all the investigating myself. I don't want to get anyone else in trouble or put them in danger."

Obadiah grimaced. "You might have a problem there."

Carsten looked up from his pancakes. "What?"

"Amos was around when your ma came to talk to me. He

heard and was headin' to talk to Edmund and Kit when I left to come here."

Carsten's mouth made an O shape but no sound. He took another bite and chewed it slowly. "I'll try to talk them out of it. I can do things on my own."

"You can, but it might be better if you all do it together."

"Why?"

"Safety in numbers. And it's easier to figure things out if you have people to talk to about it. They might have ideas you wouldn't have thought of. And might be able to ask questions you can't."

"Hm." Carsten took a bite. "I'll think about it. I don't know if I really want to involve them."

By the time they finished eating, satisfaction filled Carsten in more than one way. He now had a full belly and a more peaceful heart. He still had a lot to do and a lot of problems, but he wasn't as anxious as before. Hopefully he could talk his friends out of helping or at least get them to stay out of trouble.

CHAPTER 4

Friends

W hen he reached the farm, Carsten dismounted and handed the reins to Obadiah. "Thanks for letting me ride one of your horses. And for getting me out of jail."

"A pleasure. Don't hesitate to come see me for any advice or questions."

"Thank you." He always wavered when he had a question or needed advice. After all, he had run this farm for four years now. He should be able to figure things out on his own. Right?

Carsten watched Obadiah ride away and turned to the house. Ma should be alone in there. There was nothing to fear about going inside. So why did Carsten hesitate? He took a deep breath and headed for the door. He pushed it open and forced himself to smile so Ma would know he was all right. But it wasn't Ma he saw first.

Amos, Edmund, and Kit sat around the table. Ma stood in front of the stove, stirring something in a pot.

"Mornin'." Carsten stepped in, and all four heads swung in his direction.

Ma ran to him and pulled him into a tight hug. "I'm so glad you're all right. I was so worried about you." She let go and took a small step back to look him over. "You are all right?"

"Yes, Ma. I'm fine. I'm glad to be out, but I'm fine. What are they doin' here?" He pointed toward his three friends.

"They wanted to help you. I didn't tell them about your arrest."

"I know. Obadiah said Amos overheard you talkin' to him." Carsten gave Ma a quick squeeze and walked around her to the table. "It's nice of you to check on Ma."

"Now why didn't we think of that?" Edmund asked.

Carsten quirked an eyebrow. "What do you mean?"

Amos cleared his throat. "We didn't come to check on her. We came to wait for you to get here."

"We should o' thought of it, though," Kit said. "Next time." He winked.

Carsten rolled his eyes. "Hopefully there won't be a next time." He sat down between Amos and Kit. A plate of cookies sat on the table, and he grabbed one. "So how do you think you can help me?"

"Do you boys need me?" Ma interrupted. "The beans need to cook and can be left alone. I'd like to go out to the garden and see what I can do to get it ready for planting."

Carsten stood. "I think we've got everything we need, Ma. Thank you for the coffee and cookies."

Ma smiled. "Always happy to feed grateful boys."

Ma left, and the young men were all quiet for a couple minutes.

"What kind of help are you thinking?" Carsten asked again.

Edmund tapped the table. "By finding out who framed you for the robbery and who actually did the robbery."

Carsten looked at each of them. "I don't want to put you in danger."

Kit scoffed. "We're in danger every day. We live on

ranches and could get killed in a stampede any time. It's not likely but possible."

"What about branding season?" Carsten asked. "It's coming up next week. I don't want to keep you away from that. Your pas all need you."

"We've got hired hands," Amos said. "They want our help, and we'll do so when we can. But they know our friendship with you is important, too. They'll be fine with us helpin' you instead of them."

Kit cleared his throat. "I'll need to help Pa more than Amos does. We've only got one hired hand right now."

Edmund nodded. "We have two, but I can still help like I did in previous years."

Carsten's stomach clenched. How could he respond to these well-thought-out answers? How could he tell them he wanted to do this on his own? A second later, he realized he couldn't. Their help would be invaluable, like Obadiah had said. All Carsten had to do was give them things to do that wouldn't be dangerous. He took a deep breath. "Fine. Since I can't talk you out of it, what should we do to find the real thief?"

Silence.

"What got stolen?" Amos finally questioned.

"No idea," Carsten replied. "All I know is, it was from the print shop."

"Why do they think it was you?" Edmund questioned.

"Because I was in the shop that morning."

Kit sighed. "And the marshal can't see that you're not the same person anymore?"

"Apparently not."

"So where do we start?" Amos asked.

Carsten sighed. "I just asked that. But I don't know. Let's not worry about it today and talk about something else."

"How did you enjoy being in jail?" Edmund queried, a twinkle in his eye.

Carsten raised an eyebrow. "That's something you want to know?"

Edmund nodded, a grin on his face.

"Okay." Carsten took a minute to gather his thoughts. "It was dirty and small. Once this is all over, I'm going to see if I can find a way to make it a little better. I know it's for criminals, so it doesn't need to be luxurious, but some basic things would be nice. Like the option to have a book to read. Or have a thicker blanket. And keeping it a bit cleaner. The town can afford to hire someone to clean it every so often, and I'm sure some of the ladies in town could make quilts for each cot. Nothing fancy, just something warmer."

"That's a lot," Kit said. "What about a Bible?"

"Most criminals wouldn't read a Bible," Amos said.

"True," Kit answered, "but it's still a good thing to include."

"I agree," Carsten said.

They chatted a few more minutes before Amos stood. "I should go. Pa needs help today getting everything set up for branding."

Kit sighed. "Yeah. This time of year is always a little extra busy." He looked at Carsten. "That doesn't mean we can't help you. You are more important than the branding. So we can help whenever we're needed."

Carsten stood and walked them to the door. "Thank you for your constant friendship."

"Always," Edmund said.

Carsten's friends left, and he watched until they were out of sight. Then he went to his room. What Kit had said stuck with Carsten and reminded him that although he had recently prayed, he hadn't read his Bible in a while.

He was grateful Ma was in the garden. He didn't want her to hear him rummaging around in his room. It wasn't messy; he just didn't know for sure where he had last put his Bible.

Five minutes later, he found it half sticking out from under his bed. He used his sleeve to wipe the dust off the cover. His stomach flipped and rolled.

He sat on the bed, Bible in his hands. Where did he start? For that matter, where had he left off? He opened the Bible and found a piece of paper sticking out. He must have marked the spot at least. He turned to the paper and found the book of Ephesians. He skimmed chapters one and two and carefully read chapter three.

Paul certainly had a way with words. He made trials and tribulations seem like such good things. Peace started to fill Carsten as he continued on into chapter four. The church should be united, but how could they if they didn't forgive some people of their past sins? Sure, he'd done bad things when he was younger, but he hadn't done any stealing for four years. Couldn't they see that? Or forgive it?

As he got to verse twenty, he read slower. A Christian needed to put off the things of the old man. That made sense. Had he truly done that? He thought so but kept reading to see what Paul said. Carsten paused at verse twenty-three.

"And be renewed in the spirit of your mind; And that ye put on the new man, which after God is created in righteousness and true holiness."

That he knew he hadn't done. "God," he prayed, "I don't know how to be renewed in the spirit of my mind, so I need Your help with that. Teach me how to do it."

He went back to reading, assuming Paul probably had a few thoughts on how to renew one's mind. He did. Put away lying, speak truth to your neighbor, be angry but don't sin, don't give the devil a place in your heart. Yep. Paul had a few thoughts.

Verse twenty-eight made Carsten stop, mouth wide open. It spoke directly to him. *"Let him that stole steal no more: but rather let him labour, working with his hands the thing which is good, that he may have to give to him that needeth."*

He didn't read any farther. He had to think about this one.

35

He had stolen in the past and didn't anymore. But that last part. Sure, he worked, but only for Ma and himself. He had never thought to do something for other people.

But he could. Being the man of the house for so long meant he'd learned a lot. Including how to fix holes in the chinking and roof, make furniture, and so much more. He'd gotten pretty handy at repairing most anything. He could use those skills to help other people.

He straightened. He could find some widows who needed things fixed and offer to help them free of charge. "Thank You, God, for these verses and the idea!"

He jumped up, set his Bible on his desk, and headed outside to find Ma.

"Ma! I found something to help."

Ma stopped humming the hymn "Be Still, My Soul" and stood. "Help with what?"

He joined her in the garden. "Help people see me as a helpful person rather than a thief."

"How did you figure that out?"

"I found a verse in the Bible."

Ma smiled. "A good place to look. Come. Help me remove the weeds and tell me this idea."

Carsten knelt in the dirt with Ma and pulled a few weeds before explaining what God had shown him moments before.

Ma looked up at him, pride in her eyes. "I recommend starting with Mrs. Johnson. I was there recently, and she has leaks in her roof. She also knows most of the widows in town and can direct you to others in need."

"Then you approve?"

"Absolutely."

"Thank you, Ma."

Ma paused and looked up at him. "For what?"

"For everything. You have always supported me no matter what."

"I am doing what any good mother would."

He scooted over to her and gave her a bending-over hug. "I know. But not every mother has to raise a son on her own for the four years right before adulthood. Or deal with her son being a thief and her husband being the one who taught him. Yet through it all, you've been so patient and encouraging. It couldn't have been easy learning about Pa's way of making money when the farm wasn't doing well."

Ma straightened her back. "It wasn't. But it also wasn't completely unexpected. Your admission the year before made me suspicious of him. I'm glad he got caught when he did, or I would have had to turn him in."

Carsten ducked his head. "I should've told you long before."

"We've gone over this," Ma said, pulling his chin up with her dirty finger. "You were taught from a young age. You had no reason to mistrust your pa."

"I know."

They both went back to weeding silently.

While he pulled the annoying plants, his mind raced. Trust. It took time to build trust in people. He knew that, but what if his trust had been eroded by a person he should have been able to count on? How could he trust anyone again?

CHAPTER 5

Handyman

Carsten approached Widow Johnson's house with hesitant steps. Would she think he was crazy? Would she be willing to let him help her? He took a deep breath, set down his box of tools, and knocked on the door.

An older woman with beautiful silver hair opened. "Yes?"

"Good morning, ma'am. I'm Carsten Whitford, from church."

"Yes. I know your ma. What can I do for you?"

"I'm here to see if I can do something for you. I noticed your roof is in a bit of disrepair. I want to fix it for you. No charge."

Mrs. Johnson's eyes narrowed. "You'll do it free?"

"Yes, ma'am."

"Why?"

A glimmer of hope bloomed inside him. "I know how hard it can be to get handyman work done when there isn't a man around the house to earn money for it. I've had to learn to do a lot of things myself and want to use my knowledge to help others."

Mrs. Johnson smiled. "You brought what you need?"

"All but the cedar shingles, but I'll go get those now that I know you're willing."

"Make sure you come to the kitchen door when you finish, and I'll have a little lunch and somethin' for you to drink."

Carsten grinned. "Thank you, ma'am. I'll go on the roof to check how bad it is, then get the shingles, unless you have some."

"Check the shed out back. My late husband kept everything in there."

He picked up his tools and headed off to work.

The roof wasn't as bad as he thought it would be, and there were enough good shingles in the shed, so it only took half the day. It was nice to get away from the farmwork and do something that was physical in a different way.

After he finished, he did what Mrs. Johnson requested and knocked on the kitchen door.

"I thought the poundin' had stopped. Come in, young man. I don't have much, but you are welcome to eat whatever you want."

"Thank you, ma'am." He stepped inside the small house. It was well organized and clean. A simple lunch sat waiting for him on the table. Only one plate. He turned to Mrs. Johnson. "You aren't eating?"

"No. I ate before you came in. I didn't know you would be done so soon."

He sat at the table. The sandwich was delicious and simple. He finished it quickly so he wouldn't take up too much of Mrs. Johnson's time.

"How bad was it?"

"The roof?"

Mrs. Johnson nodded.

"Not bad, actually. I patched a few holes, removed some broken shingles, and put in the new ones. Is there anythin' else you need fixed while I'm here?"

Mrs. Johnson smiled. "You're too sweet. I don't think so but will let you know if I find somethin'."

He finished his tea. "Thank you for the food and tea, ma'am. It was very good."

Mrs. Johnson's smile became a grin. "It was my pleasure. It's a comfort to know I don't need to worry during the next rain. And I haven't cooked for others in a while either. It was nice to have someone to care for again."

Carsten stood and paused before he took a step, remembering Ma's idea about Mrs. Johnson. "Ma thought you might know of other widows who need somethin' fixed. Is she right?"

Mrs. Johnson put a hand on his shoulder and led him to the door. "She is. I don't rightly remember everyone right off, but I'll bring a list to you on Sunday."

"Thank you, ma'am. I appreciate it."

"It's the least I can do after all your help this mornin'. God bless you, son."

Carsten headed home, avoiding the town as much as possible. Helping someone as sweet as Mrs. Johnson warmed him from the inside out. He didn't want to counteract it with all the stares he knew he'd get in town.

Amos stopped in after Carsten arrived on his farm. "Hi, Carsten. Pa sent me because he told the marshal one of us would check in with you."

Carsten sighed as he ambled toward the house. "Of course the marshal would make demands like that. I'm still here and obeying everything. Thank you."

Amos looked him up and down. "You seem different."

"What do you mean?"

"You're more at peace."

Carsten smiled. "I am. I do still need to start investigating. Any ideas where to start?"

"No, but with Kit and Edmund, we could figure it out."

Carsten nodded. "I'll go tell Ma." He headed to the door as he thought of more questions. Like, who had stolen whatever it was, and what was stolen from the print shop? "Ma?" he yelled as he entered the house. "I'm headin' out to do some talkin' to Kit, Edmund, and Amos. I'll be back later today."

"Carsten Odell Whitford, you do not have to yell. I'm not deaf." She grabbed his arm before he could leave. "Aren't you gonna give your ma a hug before you go?"

He bent to embrace her. "I'll be home by supper."

"Be safe."

"I will."

Carsten and Amos headed out to the other two ranches to find their friends. They raced to the lake and swam around, splashing each other mercilessly for a while. When they'd had enough, they sat on the bank to dry off.

"It's a nice day today." Amos sighed.

"Yep," Edmund responded.

Kit spun toward Carsten. "What'd you actually bring us here for?"

"Always cutting right to it, aren't ya?" Carsten chewed his lip. "It's been a couple days since my release, and I want to know everything. But I especially want to find out what was stolen from the print shop."

"Oh, that's easy," Edmund said. "I'll go to town after we're done here and see if anyone's talkin' about it. If not, I'll ask someone what you stole. I mean, I know you didn't steal it, but everyone else thinks you're guilty. I'm sure it's all around town by now."

Carsten blinked. "You're right. Why didn't I think about that?"

Amos's hand hit his back. Hard. "That's what smart

41

friends are for. What else did you want us to figure out for you? How to solve world poverty? Done. Um... Hm. I can't think of another big issue. You get the idea."

They all laughed together.

"I'd love to come up with ways to find the real thief," Carsten said, "but I think that needs to wait until we know what got stolen."

"We could still come up with a few ideas," Amos answered.

Kit looked up at the sky. "I can't. I need to get home. I told Pa I'd help him gather all the supplies for the branding. Thanks for the cooldown. How about we meet here tomorrow after lunch to talk about other things we can do?"

"Okay," Edmund said. "See you tomorrow!" he called as Kit walked away. "If I'm gonna make it to town and back home before I'm missed too long, I should get goin'. See ya."

"And then there were two," Amos stated.

Carsten shook his head. "Yeah. But I think you need to go, too. After all, you were only meant to check in on me. Not be gone for hours."

Amos groaned dramatically as he stood. "I know. Thanks for the invite to the party."

Carsten laughed. "Glad to do it. Bye." He stood and wandered home. It was good to have friends. Ma and they were the reasons he'd stuck around the area and stayed away from stealing. He knew he couldn't lose their friendship or Ma's trust, and that had kept down the temptation to give in to the thrill. At least to a certain extent.

Now to solve this mystery so he could earn the entire town's trust.

SUNDAY, he walked with Ma to church with his head higher than normal. Not only did they know what the stolen items were, but he'd been able to help two widows this week. He felt good for the first time in a while about how people would treat him.

Edmund had learned that a stack of expensive papers had been stolen from the General Store. Which meant Marshal Lydick had lied to Obadiah and Carsten about the stolen items being from the print shop. Carsten could prove he didn't have the papers by letting the marshal search his house again as well as the barn and anywhere else he wanted to look. He planned to tell the marshal to come over whenever he wanted to look for them.

The marshal could claim Carsten had already sold them, but he had been with either his ma or his friends every minute of every day. He sighed. Except when on his own to help Widow Johnson. Surely the marshal wouldn't say all of them would lie for Carsten. Because they wouldn't. Ma was a firm believer in tough love. If he'd been guilty, she would have made him turn himself in. And his friends wouldn't lie either. They always told the truth.

Either way, it didn't matter. They had a plan to find the papers and prove his innocence. Of course, there was the problem that even if they did find the papers, they would need to convince the marshal he hadn't stolen them. That was something they would have to decide on later.

Carsten and his ma walked into the churchyard. It was already milling with people. Ma went to talk to some of the women, and he looked around to find someone. Amos was already talking to some of the other guys their age, and Luella was talking to her friends. Carsten wandered the yard looking for someone who would converse. As he did, he realized nothing had changed. When he got near, people stopped talking or changed to whispering. Their stares bored holes right through him. Even Luella turned away from him to chat to another woman.

Loneliness hit him. People all around, but no one speaking

to him. Things had not gotten better. Instead, they were worse somehow.

As he approached the steps to the church, he decided to go inside and sit until the service started. It wasn't worth waiting for someone to talk, and he suddenly didn't want to chat anyway.

He entered the empty church and went to the bench his ma and he usually sat on. Carsten stood next to it for a while and gazed unseeingly at the pulpit. *Where are You, God? Why won't You intervene? Why can't people give me the benefit of the doubt? This is all becoming too much for me. I don't know how much more rejection I can take.*

"Good morning, Carsten." A voice behind him spoke.

Carsten looked up and found Pastor Morris near him. "Mornin'." He faked a smile for the man.

"I heard it's been an eventful week for you."

Carsten nodded.

"I've been praying for you."

"Thank you." He really wanted to ask if the pastor thought he'd done it, but he didn't think that would go over well.

"How are you?"

Carsten cleared his throat. "I'm... I'm managing."

Pastor Morris smiled, making his forehead wrinkle slightly. "Good. Let me know if I can help in any way." He started walking past Carsten.

"There is one thing," Carsten said.

"Yes?"

"If..." He took a deep breath. "If, somehow, I am found guilty despite not stealing anything, please make sure Ma is taken care of."

Pastor Morris put a hand on his shoulder. "Of course. That's a job the church has. She's part of our body, so she will be well cared for."

"Thank you."

Pastor Morris went up front, and Carsten sat in the pew. People trickled in over the next few minutes.

When the bell rang, the rush was almost comical to witness from this view. Now all he had to do was enjoy the service and make it through the talking afterward.

The service was beautiful. Everyone sang so well. Of course, there were a few who didn't, but they blended in anyway. The sermon was about loving your enemies and doing good to them. Carsten knew something about that. It was a lot easier to say than to do, but it could be done with hard work.

After the service, he waited until all the women near him had left before he got up. Carsten looked around. Luella was already outside and hopefully not already talking to someone else. He needed to speak to her.

It took him a while to make his way outside. Pastor Morris made sure he shook every parishioner's hand and talked with them for a short time. Carsten appreciated that about the pastor, but today he wished he didn't have to take the time.

When it was his turn, Carsten shook the offered hand and tried to slip away quickly, but the pastor held on to his hand.

"You seem distracted today. Is there a specific way I can pray for you?"

Carsten took a quick glance around. People always gave him a wide berth, so he didn't know why he worried about eavesdroppers. "Just that I am found innocent of the theft. I didn't do it and don't know why I've been charged."

"I'll pray. God bless."

"Thank you." He escaped the steps and scanned the lawn for Luella. She was with her parents. He strode to try to intercept her before she got to them. As he neared, he called her name. She turned her head, pursed her lips, and kept walking.

Carsten watched Luella disappear with her parents. She had barely acknowledged his presence. His heart pounded as if it wanted to get out of his chest. Did she believe he had actually stolen the papers? And if she did, what did that mean for them? Were they still friends?

With slumped shoulders, he moved on and found Ma. He waited for her to finish her conversation. "Can we go home, Ma?"

Ma searched his face. "Of course. I'm sure you're starved by now anyway."

Carsten didn't have the heart to tell her that his appetite was gone.

Ma chatted most of the way home, but as they got closer, she stopped. "What's the matter, Carsten? You're never this quiet."

Carsten sighed. "I don't think Luella wants anything to do with me anymore."

"Why?"

Carsten told her what had happened.

"Maybe she was in a hurry."

Carsten shook his head. "Even when she's in a hurry, she at least takes the time to tell me. She didn't want to talk to me at all."

Ma took his arm and leaned her head on it. "I'm sorry, darling. I know how hard it is to lose the person you love. Did I tell you about the man I was in love with before I met your father?"

Carsten looked down at her. "No."

She smiled. "He was perfect. Tall, dark hair, brown eyes you could drown in."

Carsten groaned softly, and Ma laughed.

"Sorry. Too many details. We were good friends through school, and I thought he liked me. Until he married someone else. We never officially courted during our school days, so I shouldn't have had any expectations. And yet, every day after graduation, I expected him to come calling. He never did. Then I found out he was courting my best girl friend. I was so mad I didn't speak to either of them for two months. I eventually got over being mad—in time for her to ask me to be her bridesmaid."

Ma lifted her head off his arm. "My point is that it is hard to lose someone, but don't give up on her yet. If she is the one God wants you to marry, she will come around. Even though it might take a while."

"Thanks, Ma."

They reached home, and while Ma got the food out, Carsten went to his room in the loft. Up there, he made plans for how he could prove his innocence to the marshal as well as to Luella and everyone else in town.

CHAPTER 6

Luella

Sunday, March 13

Guilt gnawed at Luella. Had she really just left Carsten behind without even saying hello? Had she ever done that since the day he was in her mother's room? Probably, but not in such a rude way. She wasn't a rude person. Why had she...

She glanced over at her papa. Because of what her papa had said. Something about once a thief, always a thief. But Carsten had made drastic changes in his life. At least it seemed like he had. Maybe he was good at pretending. But all the time? Luella's chest tightened. She didn't think he could act that well.

"Luella?" Her mother's voice cut into her reverie.

Luella let out a long breath. "Yes, Mother?"

"You seemed lost in thought."

Luella forced herself to smile but knew it had to look fake. "I'm fine. I... It's been a difficult week."

Mother put her arm around Luella. "You really like that Whitford boy, don't you?"

"Mother!" Luella protested.

Mother laughed. "I don't blame you. He's a good-looking young man."

Luella shrugged. "And he's the same age as me, so a little more than just a boy."

"I knew you liked him. Why hasn't he come calling yet?"

"He just turned eighteen. He may be waiting until he's more stable financially as well. I don't know. He hasn't told me." But maybe that's what he wanted to talk about at church. She hadn't given him the chance. Luella glanced ahead as they passed the Feed and Seed Store. Her papa walked far enough in front that he couldn't hear them. "And now with this theft, he will wait at least until he gets proven innocent. Or I may need to find someone else if he's guilty."

Mother frowned. "Do you think he could be guilty?"

"No. Yes." Luella felt tears pricking her eyes. "I don't know. I'm so confused and turned around about this whole mess. I thought he'd changed. I think he has. But Papa is convinced Carsten did it. I'm not sure what to believe anymore."

"I have no idea how hard that would be. I wish I could be more help to you. I know. Let's do something fun together today. Perhaps we could make that new dress you've been wanting. And find out a way to make a matching hat."

Luella smiled. This time, it was almost real. "That is a wonderful idea. Even if we only make a new hat, that would be fine with me. That will give us time to talk as well."

"And keep your father away."

Luella giggled. "He doesn't like our chitchat, does he?"

"Or sitting around watching us sew."

They arrived at home to find a table of food the cook had prepared.

"I thought we gave her the day off," Luella said.

"We did," Papa answered. "Apparently she didn't listen again." He growled softly. "She's too loyal for her own good."

Mother nodded. "We shouldn't let the food go to waste.

Sit, please, Papa. We can complain to her tomorrow when she comes back."

Luella sat on the seat next to her mother. "Or thank her. Depending on our mood at the time." She winked, hoping it would help his grumpiness. It didn't.

Papa prayed for the food, and they ate in silence.

Before her papa could leave, Luella spoke up. "Papa, do you have any plans this afternoon?"

"I just want to be in my office by myself."

Luella smiled. "Very well. Mother and I plan to do some sewing in the parlor, if you decide you want to join us."

Papa nodded and left.

Luella stared after him. "Is it just me, or is Papa more reclusive lately?"

Mother sighed. "It isn't just you. I'm worried. Horace has only been this way once. And it took him too long to tell me what was wrong then. I don't know what to do to encourage him to open up to me this time. I don't know what made him open up to me back then."

Luella cocked her head. "When was that?"

"Before you were born. We had a few lean years. It wasn't horrible, but we were both used to wealthier living. I didn't cook well but was able to do just enough to keep us fed and healthy. I am thankful we have a cook now. And a maid. It is hard to keep up with all the household chores. I don't know how other women do it all."

Luella chewed her lip. "I don't either. But I'm hopeful I can find out someday. Assuming Carsten and I end up getting married. Of course, I'll have help from his mother. I think anyway."

Mother smirked. "I knew you liked him. I didn't know you were thinking that far ahead. You two aren't even courting yet."

"I know. But you know me, I think too far ahead on too many things. Especially when they are really important.

Which is why I have the cook teaching me how to make a variety of meals. I want to be able to cook and give Mrs. Whitford a break. Or just take over the cooking completely."

"You really do overthink. I don't think I've noticed just how much before."

Luella grinned sheepishly. "I know. It's getting bad."

"Let's go sew. Maybe while we sew, we can talk about this a little. And get you to stop thinking so hard about things that don't matter yet."

"After I clear off the table and put things away."

"I'll gather the material, needles, and thread."

"Thanks."

Luella took five trips to the kitchen and back before everything was off the table. The remaining food went into the icebox, and the dishes went in the sink. She would wash them later so Mother wouldn't have to wait too long.

LUELLA WOKE and sat straight up, heart pounding out of her chest and breath coming in gasps. A nightmare. It had only been a nightmare. Thieves weren't hanged. Unless they were horse thieves. She shuddered. No. That was no way to think right after a nightmare.

She got out of bed and stood by the window. The moon shone brightly outside. It wasn't full yet, but big enough to light up everything out there. She could see across her yard and into the neighbor's. Luella let out a sigh and turned back to her bed.

She should lie back down, but her mind and body were too awake to sleep right now. The dream had been too disturbing.

How could Carsten do this to her? To everyone? Had he stolen anything? It had been five years since she caught him in her mother's room. Since then, he seemed to have changed.

Had it all been a lie? A scheme to earn her trust? It couldn't have been. No one could be that good at deceiving everyone.

Luella rubbed her temples, a headache forming behind her eyes. It was all too much. She needed sleep. She needed clarity. And she couldn't think of a way to obtain either.

She lit a candle and opened her Bible. She read without comprehension, but even so, it helped calm her down and get her ready for going back to sleep.

When she woke up again, light streamed into the window. She sat up and rubbed her eyes. Memories from her nightmare streamed back, and she shuddered. As unsure as she was about Carsten, she didn't want to see him dead. She liked him too much. Might even love him. But she might never find out. Not if he was guilty.

CHAPTER 7
Clues

Outside Widow Eldridge's home

A week. It had been a week since the arrest. He had helped three widows so far and received meals and, from one of them, a cup of lemonade. He was content for the first time in a while. Helping them gave him increased confidence. There was one in particular who really needed the help, too.

He walked up to her house and could almost see right inside it. The chinking between the logs was almost gone. This house would only take a couple days to finish if the roof was in good shape.

He knocked.

"Can I help you?" Mrs. Eldridge asked when she saw him.

"I was actually hoping I can help you. I've been helping some of the widows in town and noticed you need a few things done to repair your house. Can I help you with that?"

"I've heard of you doin' that. Such a sweet thing to do, thank you. You're welcome to help. There's a hole in the roof over my kitchen. And I assume you saw the walls."

"I did."

Mrs. Eldridge stepped out onto the porch. "My son keeps saying he'll come do it, but he never does."

Carsten had wondered. He knew her son, Carey, worked at the print shop. Why hadn't he done this yet? "I'm happy to do it for you. There's no reason you should be freezing in here during cold nights. I'll get to work right away."

"Make sure you come in for a quick lunch, or I'll have to come out after you."

Carsten grinned. "Yes, ma'am!"

She smiled back and was about to step inside when she turned to face him again. "Oh. My late husband had some tools and materials in the shed out back. You should start there to see if he left anything that might be helpful."

"Thank you. I'll do that." Carsten started in the shed and found some chinking. Most of the tools and containers had dust on them, but there were also a few things that appeared newer or at least cleaner. Maybe Carey or Mrs. Eldridge had moved them or used them recently.

Carsten had been right in his estimation. It took a full two days to finish everything. The hole in the roof was easy. The rest took a lot of time. But Mrs. Eldridge came out and helped for a short time both days, so it went faster. If he had to guess, he'd say she helped because she wanted someone to talk to. He'd have to talk to Ma about going to visit her someday. They would both enjoy each other's company.

The last day he worked at Mrs. Eldridge's house, he stopped in at the General Store for a few things. He hadn't been there since the accusation, so he could only hope Douglas Martin would actually let him buy what he needed.

Carsten took a deep breath and went in. He browsed the shelves for the items Ma wanted. A spool of thread, some buttons, and material for a shirt for him. It didn't take long, and he brought everything to the counter.

Mr. Martin looked at him warily. "You didn't steal anything this time, did you?"

"I didn't steal anything last time either."

"You don't mind if I make sure, do you?"

"How?"

"Turn out your pockets and unbutton your shirt."

Carsten pursed his lips and did as asked. He didn't unbutton his shirt until he made sure there were no women in the store.

"How much material do you want?"

"Two yards."

Mr. Martin measured it and started cutting.

"What kind of paper did the thief steal?" Carsten asked.

"You should know."

"I don't know what kind was stolen because I didn't take anything."

"Hm."

Carsten sighed. "All I want to know is, what kind of paper? If I know that, I can help figure out who actually stole it. I want to catch the real thief. Don't you?"

"Maybe."

"Why are you so convinced I did it?"

"You have stolen in the past. Thieves usually don't reform."

"I did reform. I haven't stolen for over four years. I haven't done anything wrong for that long either." A twinge of guilt hit him. "Not anything such as stealing, for sure."

"Why should I believe you?" Mr. Martin finished cutting the cotton and folded it.

Carsten held back a growl. "I'm not the same person I was before. I'm not as selfish, and I help people now. Ask the four widows I've helped fix their houses. They were very grateful."

"It will take more than that to trust you again. I need you to pay right away upfront. No more credit."

"We never used credit anyway," Carsten said, pulling the money out.

"Your pa did."

"I'm not my pa." Carsten handed him the coins to pay for the items. Mr. Martin took them and handed Carsten the package. "Thank you. I don't suppose you'll answer my question about the paper."

Mr. Martin scowled. "It was one of the fancier papers I carry. A nice cream-colored one. Thicker than the regular paper."

Carsten smiled. "Thank you." As he headed out the store as fast as he could without running, he noticed someone behind him and looked around. The marshal. Had he been spying on him? Carsten ignored him and turned as he reached the boardwalk.

"Carsten." The marshal's voice stopped him.

"Yes?"

"I heard your questions to Douglas Martin. Be careful about investigating your own crime."

Carsten wrinkled his forehead. "Why? I'm trying to figure out who stole from him! Which is also what you should be doing."

"I did find the guilty person."

"Then where is the paper I stole? You didn't find anything when you searched my house."

"You could have hidden it anywhere before I got there."

Carsten scoffed. "Where am I going to hide paper without the possibility of it getting ruined except in the house?"

"I don't know. Thieves aren't always known for their smarts."

"Maybe. But smart thieves don't get caught. And I'm not known for being stupid." That, at least, was true. No one had accused him of being stupid.

"Be careful, Carsten. I'm keeping a close eye on you."

Carsten gritted his teeth. "Yes, sir. I'll be careful."

He waited until the marshal went back to his office before he headed for home. What had that been about? Why would he be so concerned about Carsten looking into this? Especially when the marshal basically admitted he wasn't going to look into it.

The encounter proved there was no way anyone in town would see him as anything but a thief. Thankfully, with fancy paper, it would be too expensive to burn the evidence, which meant the thief was using it now or had it hidden away.

But who else would have stolen it? Carsten had to find out. And within the next three weeks or so, before the judge came to town.

Carsten almost ran into the front door before he realized he had made it home. He placed the items on the table for Ma to take care of and headed out to the field.

He grabbed a hoe from the barn and wandered the alfalfa field, hoeing weeds when he saw them. But mostly, he prayed.

"God, I don't know what to do. If Ma and Luella weren't here, I'd sell the farm and move away after the trial. I don't want to leave my friends, but I can't live forever someplace the people don't trust me. I know I need to trust You more, but I don't know how to do that."

Carsten stopped. He should search the Bible about trust. He would do that tonight. Right now, he needed to get back to his prayer and alfalfa.

"God, there's another matter we need to talk about. Even with this crop doing better now, I don't think there will be enough money to pay for the seed we need for the next crop. I have some seed I saved from last year, and it will grow again, just not as lush. And I want to try something new for Mr. Raskins.

"I know Pa stole to be able to pay for the lean years, but I can't, and won't, do that. I need to find a second job to help pay our extra expenses. And preferably one that won't take too much time away from the fields. Thank You. I know You can do all things, and right now, I need some of that. Amen."

He hoed the weeds out of a third of the field and stood looking at it. The crop wasn't as lush as in previous years, but it would do. He took a deep breath and headed to the house. He needed Ma's wisdom and advice on finding a job in town. Maybe she'd have some ideas.

AFTER CHURCH THE NEXT WEEK, he exited the building during the final prayer. He wanted to make sure to at least try to talk to Luella. He needed to tell her he didn't do this. He needed to explain himself. He waited until she came down the stairs of the church and approached her. "Luella."

"I have nothing to say to you," Luella said. She turned to leave.

Carsten took a step closer. "I know. But I have to tell you that I didn't do this crime. Your mother's necklace was the last thing I ever attempted to steal." Was that a lie? The palomino... He couldn't think about that now. "Please believe me."

Luella spun his direction. "I can't." He saw a tear in her eye. "I can't. Not yet. I want to. But..." She looked up and took in a deep breath. "If they prove you innocent, then I'll believe. Truly."

She hurried off before he could say another word. Carsten stared after her. Why couldn't she believe him? What held her back? He wandered home in a daze.

It wasn't until he reached the front door that he realized he hadn't waited for Ma. He headed back to the road and found her almost to their home already, chatting with Mrs. Eldridge.

"Carsten! Look who I talked into coming home with me."

He put on an almost genuine smile. "Mrs. Eldridge. It is good to see you. How is the chinking holding up?"

Mrs. Eldridge pulled him into a tight hug. "Perfect. It is so nice to not have a breeze coming through the walls all the time. Especially at night. Thank you, my boy."

"I was happy to do it."

That afternoon sped by faster than he anticipated. Mrs. Eldridge's visit helped a lot. As he walked back from taking her to her home, he thought about how close the trial must be. Only a couple more weeks, maybe up to three, and he had nothing to prove his innocence. It was time to change that.

CHAPTER 8
Work

"Trust in the Lord with all thine heart; and lean not unto thine own understanding."

Carsten had read that verse from Proverbs two days earlier, and it still ran through his mind over and over again. He knew what it meant, of course. That was easy. But actually putting it into practice? Not easy at all. While he walked to town, he thought about how he could logically apply the verse to his situation. He could trust that God would prove his innocence, but how? Carsten didn't know if he could do that without doing something to help God along. Didn't God need humans to help Him sometimes?

Carsten sighed. Being a Christian was harder than he thought it would be. Worth it, of course, but hard.

He reached town and put on a more neutral face. One that said he didn't care what people said about him. Even though he did. It bothered him when they ignored him or acted as if he didn't know they were talking about him. He went straight to the print shop. When he had made his order, they had told him to come in two weeks later. It hadn't quite been two weeks, but he decided to check anyway.

Carsten took a deep breath as he opened the print shop door. No one was out front. He went to the counter and looked around. No one. He was about to leave when he heard voices.

"It won't work. I've tried everything."

"Are you sure?"

"Positive. I tried different papers, different inks. Everything I can think of. Well, short of taking the whole thing apart."

There was a bang and a curse word from Mr. Graves. "We can't run this store on hand-printed items! What could have happened? It worked fine last night, before we left."

"I know."

Carsten chewed his lip and stepped around the counter and into the back room. "Excuse me."

Mr. Graves turned, a fake smile on his face. "Carsten. I have your print..."

"Thanks, but I actually came to the back room to see if I can help. I heard you talking about the press not working." Carsten quirked a sheepish smile. "I've gotten good at figuring out machinery and fixing problems. One of the perks of not being able to afford paying for help from someone else. I won't do anything unless I think it will actually help."

Relief flooded Mr. Graves's face. "That would be much appreciated. Thank you."

"But he's a thief!" Carey Eldridge exclaimed. "Are you sure you want him here?"

"He *was* a thief and is currently accused," Mr. Graves said. "A man is innocent until proven guilty. So far, I haven't heard of anything that proves for sure he is guilty. And if he can help, it will be worth anything he may or may not steal out of here."

"I assure you," Carsten said, "I won't steal anything. All I want to do is help." He approached the press and looked it over. It was a fairly simple design. Levers for adjusting the paper thickness, plates for pressing ink into the paper, and ink for pressing onto plates.

Wait. Ink.

He looked closer at the ink. Red ink caked in the spot where the paper should have fed through. It was well hidden and in a place no ink should be. No wonder they had missed it.

"Do you have any rags and water? I also need all the paper out of the press."

"I'll be right back." Mr. Graves left the room.

"You better be careful," Carey hissed. "I'm watching every move you make. I won't let Mr. Graves get stolen from."

"I'm not here to steal anything. I'm here to fix your press so you can have some work to do. And pick up the print I ordered."

"Did you steal anything when you ordered your print? That's the day you stole from the General Store, isn't it?"

Carsten sighed. "I didn't steal from the General Store."

"Everyone says you did."

"I know. But I didn't." He desperately wanted to ask why Carey didn't help out his mother more. Even as Carsten thought it, he knew it would get him angrier, and he didn't want to make Carey more of an enemy.

Mr. Graves came back before Carey could say anything else.

"Thank you," Carsten said. He took the rag and bucket of water and cleaned the ink off the press. It took some hard scrubbing, but it finally came off. He stood and stretched. "Try it now."

Carey and Mr. Graves did their magic getting paper and ink set up and ran a sample through the machine.

Mr. Graves approached Carsten with an outstretched arm and a huge grin on his face. "Thank you. What can I do to repay you? You have saved me at least a day's worth of work.

First, you are getting your print for free. No need to pay me. No negotiations there. Other than that, how much should I pay you?"

Carsten's breath caught. Maybe this was the answer to his prayer. "Actually, I have something else in mind."

"What's that?"

"Do you happen to need another employee? Someone who can work flexible hours and will be more available in the winter than the other months?"

Mr. Graves raised his eyebrows and nodded. "I could do that. You need a little extra income?"

"Yes, sir."

"What would you think of doing deliveries? Some of my customers live farther away and don't get into town often. I could offer to deliver their products to them so they don't have to come all this way."

"What?" Carey protested. "What if he's found guilty?"

Mr. Graves put a hand on Carey's shoulder. "Then he's out of a job anyway. I'm willing to take a chance on him after his help here."

Hope sprang up. Could it be that Carsten had finally found a shop owner who believed in him? "Thank you for the chance, Mr. Graves. When should I start? And how much are you thinking of paying?"

Mr. Graves led him out to the front of the store. "Does two dollars per delivery sound fair? I have at least one print that needs delivered this week, if you can come in sometime."

"Sure. How big is it? I don't have a wagon. Just a horse."

"That should be fine. If we need something bigger, I can always rent a wagon from the livery for that day. I don't know how busy you are with your farm, but perhaps you could stop in once a week to see if we need you."

"Until the alfalfa needs harvesting, I would be able to have at least a couple afternoons free each week."

"Great! I'll get your print so you can take it home with you."

"Thank you."

Mr. Graves disappeared into the back for a minute but returned shortly with a small print. "What do you think?"

Carsten looked at it. There were two different fonts for the verse, one fancier and one plain. It was beautiful. "Ma will love this."

"You're welcome. I'll see you later this week."

"Yes, sir."

As Carsten left, he saw Carey standing in the back doorway, glaring at him. Why was he so against Carsten's having this job? On the surface, it would appear the fellow wanted to save his boss from a criminal, but it seemed like more than that.

Carsten shook his head. What Carey thought of him didn't really matter. Mr. Graves was the owner and could run his shop however he saw fit.

A familiar scent reached Carsten's nose. It was the telltale smell of lavender and orange blossoms from Luella's perfume. He looked around and tried to find her. She wasn't anywhere in sight, though. Maybe she had ducked into a store. With a sigh, he moved on. It would have been nice to show her the print since she had helped him so much with it, but he didn't have time or energy to try to find her.

On his way home, he stopped by Amos's house.

"Carsten! How's it goin'?"

"Not too bad. I got a job in town."

Amos blinked. "What?"

Carsten smirked. "I need something so we don't go into debt next year. It's only a day or two a week. But it means I might be busier and not able to investigate as much."

"Ah. And you want me to tell Kit and Edmund you won't be around as much."

"If you can."

"Sure. I wanted to see them today anyway. See how branding is going for them."

"Thanks. Give them my best!"

"I will."

CHAPTER 9

Ranger

Dallas, Texas

L onzo Hossman strode down the street to the Texas Rangers' office, a grin plastered on his face. His first day as a Ranger and only twenty-one. Life couldn't get more exciting than this. He opened the door and blinked a few times, trying to get his eyes to adjust to the dim light inside.

"You must be Ranger Hossman."

Lonzo, still unable to see more than her shape, nodded. "I'm here to see Captain Bertram."

"Have a seat." The dark-haired woman pointed to a chair near her desk. "He'll be right with you."

Lonzo's eyes finally adjusted to the light, and he settled onto the wooden chair. This wasn't as exciting as he'd hoped, but he supposed his job wouldn't always be exciting. He looked around the room, closed his eyes, and gave himself thirty seconds to list fifteen things he saw and where they were. He did it twice before the door opened.

A tall, well-tanned man stood in the doorway. "Lonzo!" His voice boomed through the room. "Come in, come in. I have a job for you today."

Lonzo stood and followed the large man into his office. "Thank you, sir. I'm happy to do anything."

Captain Bertram chuckled as he dropped onto his chair. "Of course you are. Today's job is simple. Sit down."

Lonzo sat on a padded wooden chair. "What's the job?"

"There's a young woman in town who is meeting up with a man who claims to be her father. Her mother never told her anything about him, and she recently inherited a tidy sum from her grandfather."

"You are suspicious of the timing."

Captain Bertram tapped his fingers on the desk. "He's a man down on his luck and not the most reputable. I need you to escort the young lady to the meeting and tell me what you think of him. Miss Amelia has given permission for you to ask questions, if you have any. You will meet her at her home at ten thirty, and she will tell you where to go from there."

"You don't know where the meeting is?"

"No."

"But she asked for your help with this?"

Captain Bertram sighed. "Not exactly. She told a friend of mine, and he requested I send someone to help her. I talked to Miss Amelia, and she agreed." He handed Lonzo a piece of paper.

Lonzo took a look at the paper. It was the address. "Should be an interesting first day."

"More than mine," the captain said with a laugh. "I had to follow my boss around all day while he talked to people."

Lonzo chuckled. "Sounds thrilling."

"As he said, it was good to see that not every day would be chasing desperadoes. We've got plenty of dull days as well. The sooner you accept that, the better."

"Yes, sir."

Captain Bertram glanced up. "It's time for you to go meet Miss Amelia. I'm sure she'll have something she wants to tell you. Since becoming an heiress, she's gotten rather opin-ionated."

Lonzo grinned. "I grew up with an older sister who was the same way, but she wasn't an heiress. I think I can handle Miss Amelia."

"You sound more than equipped to. Good luck, Lonzo. And when you finish, come back here so I can show you how to write the reports and file them."

"Yes, sir." Lonzo stood and walked out of the office, then out of the building. He stopped outside the door. The light was blinding. Why was it so dark in that building? When his eyes adjusted, he started down the boardwalk. The address was in the rich part of town. Full of huge, fenced-in mansions.

It would take a bit of a walk to get there, but he had plenty of time. Could this man really be her father, or was it someone who wanted her money? He would need all his discernment for this one.

"God, I'm thankful for this job and that You directed me to it. I need Your help today, though. This one will be hard to figure out. The man might be honest, or he might be a fraud. I'm not sure how I'll be able to tell. Give me guidance, please. I could use some patience as well. You know I lack patience many times, and I'll need it a lot in this job, especially today."

He turned a corner and stopped both movement and prayer. The houses were massively bigger than anywhere else in the town. Or anywhere that he'd seen.

Lonzo looked at the paper again and found the house two doors down. The fence and yard were in mild disrepair compared to the rest of the neighborhood. Captain Bertram had said Miss Amelia was a recent heiress. Maybe the relative who had died had let things get out of hand before she inher-ited. He pushed the gate, and it creaked open. Shouldn't her servants have cared for this? Or were there other priorities she had made instead?

He took a deep breath and walked up to the ivy-over-grown door. With a slight raise of his eyebrows, he pushed a branch out of the way and grabbed the knocker. He hit it three times and heard it echo through the room. No furniture to deaden the noise? Or a really big room?

Lonzo waited a full minute before hearing footsteps.

"Sorry!" was the first word out of the disheveled young woman's mouth as she opened the door. "I was upstairs cleaning when I heard the knock. My sister, Amelia, will be down momentarily. She was finishing up getting dressed after cleaning with me all morning. We decided it would be best if one of us met with our possible father, and I really don't need to tell you all of this. I talk when I get nervous. Sorry." She grimaced, and a lock of hair, escaping from her bun, fell onto her face. "Again. Won't you come in? We don't have much right now. The servants took advantage of our grandfather's poor health and stole nearly everything as well as keeping things filthy, except Grandpa's room."

Lonzo stepped into the large, empty entryway. "I'm used to messes. I have four sisters, which you would think meant our house could be spotless. Not with these four. They fought over who should do the cleaning more than they actually cleaned. My name is Lonzo Hossman. I'm a Texas Ranger."

"Emmeline Wilso—I mean, Emmeline Massey. Our name was Wilson until our grandfather's private investigator discovered who Ma really was. Then he adopted us and changed our name. We're still not used to it."

"Who was your ma, and why did she not tell you about your grandfather?"

"I'll get to that later. Or let my sister fill you in, actually," Emmeline said.

Lonzo nodded. "It's a pleasure to meet you, Miss Emmeline. Have you and Miss Massey thought of hiring someone to help you?"

"Oh, we have, but we haven't figured out where to go to find good servants."

"Can your neighbors help?"

Miss Emmeline giggled. "Our neighbors are appalled that two country hicks inherited this place and that the private investigator would dare think a single mom could possibly be Mr. Massey's daughter."

"Did the investigator talk to your ma?"

"He wanted to, but she passed on a year before he came around. We did find evidence that he was right, though."

"Which is immaterial now," a new voice said. A well-dressed woman, a few years older than Emmeline, stood at the bottom of the stairs. "I'm Amelia. You must be the Texas Ranger dear Adam Bertram requested I take with me."

Lonzo held out his hand. "Lonzo Hossman. Is there anything else you want to add to our conversation? Perhaps about any evidence of who your pa is?"

"All I know is that Ma refused to talk about him. Her pa disowned her after she learned she was expecting me. She went off to live in a small town in western Texas when Emmeline was born. We asked many times about Pa, but she never shared details." Amelia sighed. "The only evidence we found was the family Bible Ma had. When we looked in it, we found the family tree where Ma's mother had written in Ma's name as Belle Massey. Under it were our names but no father."

"How old were you when Emmeline was born?"

"Three," Emmeline butted in. "She doesn't remember anything."

Amelia smiled sadly. "I wish I did. It would make today much easier. If I could even remember a glimpse of his face." She looked up at the clock. "I have no idea what time it is since that thing is still broken, but I'm guessing we need to leave."

Lonzo pulled out his pocket watch. "Yes, we should. Where are we headed?"

"A small café near the Rangers' office."

Lonzo raised an eyebrow.

"Yes, I chose it for that reason." She turned to her sister. "I'll be back as soon as I can. Don't feel like you have to clean while I'm gone. I know how much you hate it."

Emmeline giggled. "I may hate cleaning, but I hate sitting around doing nothing more. Keep her safe, Mr. Hossman."

"I will," Lonzo said with a chuckle. He offered Amelia his arm, and she took it gently. "What shall we talk about on our walk?"

"What questions to ask this man to determine if he is our father?"

"Do you know how your mother met him?"

"Yes."

Lonzo smiled. "Then ask where they met. If he answers correctly, we move on to harder questions. Does he already know about your sister?"

"Not that I am aware."

"Then ask something about his son. Throw him off. If he really knew your mother well, he should have at least known she had a girl, not a boy, if your mother waited to leave until after Emmeline was born."

Amelia gripped his arm a little tighter. "You are good at this."

"Thank you."

"If he still answers correctly, we should ask him more about if they were married, and if so, why Ma left. More for my own curiosity, but it might also give some explanations that I want to know myself. If he is truly the man he claims to be."

Lonzo chewed his lip. "How are you going to introduce me?"

"As a family friend. I thought of saying you were my fiancé but didn't think we should do anything that elaborate."

"'Family friend' works for me. One question I didn't want to ask in front of Emmeline. Are you sure she has the same father as you?"

"Ma never said otherwise, but I don't know for sure."

Lonzo nodded. "Is there anything I need to know before we go in?"

Amelia slowed for a step. "I can get a little contentious and might need you to help me tone it down some."

"I will do what I can."

They approached the café and went inside. Amelia looked around the room. "He isn't here yet."

"Let's go ahead and sit down facing the door so you can see when he gets here."

When Amelia detached her arm from Lonzo's, he noticed her hand shook. She looked confident except for that slight shakiness. If this man was truly who he claimed, she might finally be getting answers for the first time in her life. Lonzo had no idea how hard that had to be if you didn't even know who your father was or why your mother left him.

Lonzo sat next to her, keeping a careful eye on everyone who sat nearby and entered the café. Nothing was going to happen to Amelia on his watch.

A man walked in and glanced around. Amelia straightened and stood. Lonzo hurried to stand as well, and the man came over, looking at Lonzo with concern. "Amelia, thank you for agreeing to meet." He held out his hand.

Amelia shook his hand. "This is a family friend, Lonzo Hossman. I asked him to come along."

"Nice to meet you. I'm Gary Wilson."

Lonzo shook the man's offered hand. "Pleasure. Wilson?"

"Yes. Amelia's mother and I were married."

Amelia cleared her throat. "Let's sit so the waitress can take our order. Then we can talk."

"Of course," Mr. Wilson said.

Lonzo ordered a coffee. He wasn't hungry.

Once the waitress left, Amelia spoke up. "How did you and Ma meet?"

Mr. Wilson blinked slowly. "Right to it. We met at a dance.

She was the prettiest young woman there. We talked and danced, and for some reason, she seemed to really enjoy spending time with me. I liked her, too, and said so. She told me her father would never approve of a man of my little means, but she wanted to keep seeing me."

Amelia leaned in. "And you still decided to see her again?"

"Yes. We met in public places but none that your grandfather would go to. We fell in love. Belle tried to talk to her father about me. He didn't take it well and threatened to disown her if she did anything stupid such as marry me.

"We discussed everything, and she was willing to live the way I did. I proposed, and we got married. None of her family or friends were there, but they were invited, and my family welcomed her with open arms." Mr. Wilson got quiet.

"Why did she leave you and never tell us who you are?" Amelia asked.

Mr. Wilson sighed. The waitress came with their orders, and he waited to answer until she left. "Her father had disowned her four years earlier. Then suddenly he came to see her while she was expecting your sister. I don't know what he said, but it upset her, and the next day, she went into labor and had Emmeline."

Amelia glanced at Lonzo and gave a slight smile.

"Whatever he said stuck with Belle, and she barely talked to me until the day she left. She said something about knowing what I'd done. All I can assume is that her father made up a lie about me being unfaithful to her. When she and Emmeline were strong enough, she took you two and disappeared. I didn't have the money to go searching long or the courage to confront your grandfather. I have been utterly ashamed of myself since then."

Lonzo cleared his throat. "What did you do to try to find her?"

Mr. Wilson stared at the wall. "I asked around at the train

station, stage station, and livery. No one admitted to seeing a woman, a three-year-old, and a newborn. I asked everyone I could think of. Women seemed afraid of me, even her friends; men refused to make eye contact. It was horrible. I couldn't get a soul to talk to me. So I went on to other surrounding towns to see if any of them knew anything. Nothing. I traveled as far as I could but never found her. I stayed in western Texas and asked my parents to sell my house for me. I couldn't live in a town where people suspected me of something."

Amelia, tears streaking down her cheeks, leaned forward and took his hand. "Why are you just now coming forward with this?"

Mr. Wilson shook his head. "It wasn't until I heard your grandfather died and had two granddaughters named as his heirs that I even knew you were here. I came back to town as soon as the news hit. I needed to see you two again. Even if you never wanted to see me. I didn't care. I needed to see how you two turned out."

Amelia smiled at Lonzo. "He is really our father. Thank you for coming and keeping me safe. I want to bring him home to meet Emmeline."

Lonzo took the last drink of coffee from his cup, put a few coins on the table, and stood. "It was a pleasure meeting you, Mr. Wilson. Good day, Miss Massey."

Lonzo stepped out onto the street, a grin on his face. Now to find out what kind of paperwork he needed to fill out about this.

CHAPTER 10

Kit

K it sat on his bed, resting his chin in his hand, a frown on his face. Carsten's trial was in as little as two weeks or as much as three. They needed to find something. Edmund and Amos had helped him talk to people around town the last few days. Nothing. No one was talking about who else the thief could be. Everyone seemed convinced it had to be Carsten.

But they didn't know him like the Three *Amigos* did. The townspeople hadn't seen how Carsten had gone from a selfish boy who used to talk about himself almost constantly to a selfless young man who helped the less fortunate.

There was the time Carsten had helped him find the lost calf during harvesttime. Not many farmers would have risked losing their crop to help a rancher find one little calf. That had been a hot, hard, but fun day.

Kit shook his head. He needed to leave now or he wouldn't be back for supper.

He slid off the bed and headed downstairs and out the door. "I'll be in town for a while, Ma."

"No candy today," she called from the kitchen. "Too much

will spoil you. Besides, I'm making a cake for supper, so you'll have sweets later."

Kit sighed. He would always be a child to Ma, even though he could be living on his own now if he wanted. "Yes, ma'am." He ran down the road until he reached the magnolia tree. At the fork in the road, he glanced up the other side and wondered what Carsten was up to. He couldn't take the time to find out today. Pa needed this branding iron tomorrow.

Kit walked toward town and entered the General Store. In the store, he went straight to the counter. "Excuse me," he said to Mr. Martin. "I'm lookin' for another branding iron. Do ya have any left?"

Mr. Martin quirked his mouth. "Not sure. Let me check in back."

"Thanks."

Kit browsed the candies on the counter. His sweet tooth made his mouth water, but he kept his hands away from the jars. He needed to keep his promise to his ma.

"Got two left," Mr. Martin said as he emerged from the back. "You want both or one?"

"One, please."

"Anythin' else?"

"Nope. That's all."

Mr. Martin named the price, and Kit handed him a five. Mr. Martin gave him change back, and Kit took the money and pole. "Thanks, Mr. Martin. See ya Sunday."

"See you then."

Kit stuffed the money back into his pocket and headed out. He was about to turn home when he heard his name.

Luella hurried in his direction.

"Can I help you with somethin', Miss Comstock?"

"How's Carsten doing?" Her face twisted in concern.

Kit narrowed his eyes. "Don't you two talk a lot?"

"I…" She looked away. "I've been avoiding him since the arrest."

"Why?"

Luella looked down. "I'm afraid he's guilty. I don't know who to believe anymore about all this. I want to believe he didn't do it, but everyone is saying it had to be him."

"It wasn't."

She glanced up with pleading eyes. "How do you know?"

"I know him. He's changed in recent years. Especially since his pa was put in prison. He wouldn't steal anything. He even got a job so he can pay for new seed this fall."

"He did?"

Kit nodded.

Luella bit her lip. "I don't know. I'll think about that. I just don't know if I can trust him yet. But you never did answer my question."

"He's fine. Besides everyone thinkin' he stole the papers. Including his girl, apparently."

Luella's face became red. "I…" She paused and swallowed hard. "How can you be so sure he is innocent?"

Kit crossed his arms as best he could with a pole in one hand. "The only reason he stole before is because his pa taught him and he wanted to prove himself to his pa. Like all boys do. But most pas aren't thieves. Besides that, did you know he's been fixing things for widows?"

"I've heard talk about it but didn't know for sure. Why?"

"He wants to. He knows his ma would have a hard time keepin' everything nice if he wasn't around. So he goes around and tries to find at least one widow a week to help."

"For pay?"

"No. He refuses money. He'll take a meal but nothin' else."

Luella chewed her lip. "Hm. Maybe Papa was wrong."

Kit was about to ask what she meant, but Luella said her goodbyes and left before he could.

He shook his head at the suddenness of her departure and headed back to the ranch. As he did, he stuck his free hand in his pocket. Something made him stop. Kit took the bill out and looked at it. It looked normal but also not quite right. But why wouldn't it be?

He put it in the opposite pocket of the coins he'd gotten back so he wouldn't accidentally give the dollar to his pa. Maybe his friends could help figure out why it was different. And even if they couldn't, maybe they could tell him whether he was imagining things.

CHAPTER 11

Purpose

"Why did you get us together so urgently, Kit?" Carsten asked as they gathered in Kit's ma's kitchen.

Kit fished something out of his pocket. "I need to show you something. And I need you to tell me if I'm crazy about this."

Amos narrowed his eyes. "Why would you be crazy?"

"I got this money in town. Something seems different about it, but I can't figure out what. Did you all bring your dollar bills?"

Carsten, Amos, and Edmund all nodded.

"Good. Give them to me, and I'll shuffle them up. Then you can each try to figure out which is mine."

Carsten handed his dollar bill to Kit and watched as Amos and Edmund did as well.

Kit mixed them up and laid them down on the table. "Which is the one I put in?"

Carsten let Amos and Edmund go first. They looked at each bill thoroughly and pushed them over to him. Carsten started at one corner and checked the top first, then the bottom, setting each down after he finished.

"Well?" Kit asked.

"Number three," Amos answered.

"I agree," Edmund said.

"Me, too," Carsten replied. "I think it might be a different paper."

"But why?" Amos asked. "Why would it be different?"

"I don't know."

Carsten picked up Kit's money and rubbed it between his fingers again, staring at it the whole time. "I..." He paused, gathering his thoughts. "I've heard of people making money. They call it... counterfeit."

"As in, not real at all?" Kit asked. "I have a worthless dollar bill? What will I tell Pa?"

Amos patted his back. "Once we solve this, your pa will understand and not blame you at all. So, the money is fake. Why would someone make fake money?"

Carsten shrugged. "If it was good enough, you could technically get rich doing this. And it seems they've got it pretty good. Could someone from out of town have left it? If not, who in town would benefit from something like this? And why? I would think there would have to be more than one person involved. A mastermind and a worker. Maybe? But what could they get out of this partnership?"

"Maybe they are having money troubles," Amos said.

"Obviously," Kit said. "But—"

"Why 'obviously'?" Carsten interrupted. "Don't the rich usually want to get richer? And wouldn't they need someone to pay for the equipment? Not that I think any of the well-to-do people here are doing this, but it's something to think about."

Kit shrugged. "I suppose. But around here, it's more likely to be someone with money troubles. Which also implicates you to an extent, Carsten. Except we know you better than that."

Carsten sighed. His friend was right.

"But," Kit continued, "as I was saying, I think whoever is doing this needs a deeper motivation than money troubles."

"Do we really need to figure out the motive?" Edmund asked.

Amos paced from the stove to the table. "No. But should we even try to find out who they are?"

"Why wouldn't we?" Edmund asked, face lighting up.

Carsten pursed his lips. "It could be dangerous. There could be more people involved, and this isn't what we planned to do. Unless they set me up to take the fall for the counterfeiting, too."

"Which they probably did," Kit said. "And even if they didn't, if there are people making counterfeit money, we need to find out who they are so we can tell the authorities."

"Or tell the authorities now, and they can find the people," Carsten suggested.

"But what authorities?" Amos asked. "I don't trust the marshal."

"I don't either," Carsten said. "But it would be safer than us investigating on our own."

"And if the marshal is part of it?" Kit asked. "If he knows we're onto him, he could come after us."

"True," Amos said. "We should look into it before we tell anyone."

Carsten sank onto a nearby chair. His job. If there was counterfeiting going on, at least one of the men at the print shop had to be involved. A printing press bought by anyone except Mr. Graves would have been suspicious. Could that be why the machine suddenly didn't work that one day?

"Is something wrong, Carsten?" Amos asked.

"No," Carsten responded too quickly. He pursed his lips. "Well, probably not. I might lose my job if we keep investigating."

"What job?" Edmund asked.

Kit turned to Edmund. "He makes deliveries for the print shop."

Edmund raised his eyebrows. "Right. Do you still help the widows?"

"A little," Carsten said. "I've only made one delivery so far, so I still have some time to help one widow a week. I'm running out of widows to help, though. And it was only a temporary idea. Not something I was going to do all the time."

"If you do lose your job, you could hire out as a handyman," Amos said.

"I suppose." Carsten took a deep breath. "So how do we find the counterfeiters?"

"Who would be corrupt enough or desperate enough to benefit from having extra money?" Kit asked.

Amos scoffed. "Almost everybody in town. We're not exactly known for rich people around here. Well, except Pa and I, I suppose."

"People who are heavily in debt," Edmund said. "But they would be about as hard to find as figuring out who the counterfeiters are."

Kit handed the real money back to each of them. "Let's take time to think about it and gather at the lake in two days."

"Good idea," Carsten said. He left first. He needed to be alone. Fake money, fake accusations. His mind spun in circles. His pace got faster and faster the longer he went. He didn't want to show his friends how much this new revelation affected him.

Pieces from his past and present started to fit together. Getting caught by Luella five years before had saved him a lifetime in jail with his father. And had made him talk to Ma about eternal salvation.

And now? Now he was accused of a robbery he didn't do, and him and his friends had the chance to catch criminals who were worse than robbers. Is that what God had planned?

Had God allowed Carsten to be falsely accused so he could find the true criminals in this town?

He made it home and went straight into the field. He couldn't talk to Ma right now. Not until he sorted a few things out. Why had all this talk of counterfeiting brought up his past? Were there things he hadn't fully dealt with? If so, how did he figure that out?

He stopped in the middle of a row of alfalfa. "God, I don't know what to do. I've got things I need to take care of, but I don't know how. I still feel guilty about the horse I borrowed. Was I the cause of the owner's death? I don't know. I also don't know how to discourage my friends from helping me more. I don't want to endanger their lives. When we were only going after a thief, it was dangerous enough. But now?" He sighed.

"Are the counterfeiters dangerous? Do I need to find someone else to take over the investigation? I don't know. Help me, God. I need You. I don't know what to do anymore."

Carsten left the prayer at that, grabbed a hoe, and went to work on the alfalfa. He'd neglected it a bit the past couple days while he worked in town and then met with his friends. The weeds were getting a bit bigger than he liked, so he took a hoe to them, working out his frustration on them. The burn in his muscles somehow helped soothe the pain in his heart.

After a couple hours, he stopped to catch his breath. His vision went a little dark around the edges, and he sucked in a deep breath, which led to him coughing hard. His parched throat felt like sandpaper. No wonder his head spun. He had worked hard under a hot sun without any water.

He stumbled out of the field to the well in their backyard. He pulled the bucket up and dumped it over his head to cool himself off. With a deep sigh of contentment, he sent the bucket down for more water. This time, he drank deeply and sat on the edge of the well, gazing out at the field.

When had the field gotten lusher? A couple weeks ago, the field worried him. But then he set the worry aside to concentrate on the accusations against him.

Maybe that's what he needed to do. He needed to set aside the guilt of borrowing the horse those four years ago. It had been a childish fantasy to ride a palomino and steal the horse. Something he needed to get past. In all likelihood, he hadn't been the cause of the owner's death. He needed to get over it. But how?

Carsten sighed. It was definitely easier said than done.

Suppertime was close, so he decided not to go back out to the field. Hopefully Ma wouldn't be too nosy and talkative today. He wasn't sure he wanted to converse much. But maybe discussing things with her would help.

How did one find counterfeiters? Was there a way to know who was making the counterfeit money and using it?

THE NEXT DAY, Carsten rode their aging mare, Sarai, to the print shop.

Mr. Graves met him outside. "I've got a delivery today. Do you know where Old Man Jenkins lives?"

"Can't say as I've met him, but I've been past the place. My friends and I used to make up stories about him."

Mr. Graves chuckled. "Most kids do, I think. This is Mr. Jenkins's." He handed over the rolled-up paper.

Carsten quirked an eyebrow. A hermit who ordered a print? "I'll get it to him. Anything else?"

"Nah. You can go do whatever you like after. Here's your pay."

Carsten took the money and unconsciously rubbed it to see if he could tell if it was counterfeit. "More than fair. Thank you, sir. When should I come next?"

"Stop by early next week. I've got another item that should be ready by then."

"All right. See you then."

"Take care, Carsten."

Carsten carefully strapped the print to his saddlebag and swung up onto Sarai. The ride out to the Jenkins place was pleasant and soothing. He'd been in such turmoil yesterday and even this morning that he needed a little time doing something different. He hummed Be Still, My Soul and as he reached the second verse started singing.

> Be still, my soul: thy God doth undertake
> To guide the future, as He has the past.
> Thy hope, thy confidence let nothing shake;
> All now mysterious shall be bright at last.
> Be still, my soul: the waves and winds still know
> His voice Who ruled them while He dwelt below.

As he got near the Jenkins place, he paid keen attention, knowing his friends would want an accounting of everything.

Trees surrounded the place, but there was a path through them onto which he led Sarai. They came out into a small clearing, and he saw a small log cabin. Built on the side was a stone chimney.

Carsten let out a small breath. He saw something out of the corner of his eye and turned his head. An older man ran toward him with a rifle. His heart jumped into his throat, and he dismounted, keeping Sarai between Mr. Jenkins and himself.

"Mr. Jenkins, I'm delivering your print from the print shop."

"Graves didn't say there'd be a delivery. How do I know you're tellin' the truth?"

Carsten unstrapped the print from the saddlebag and stepped away from Sarai, holding the print in one hand and both hands up in the air. "This is your print." He let it unroll so Mr. Jenkins could see what he had ordered.

Mr. Jenkins lowered his rifle so it faced the ground. "I'm sorry. I didn't know who you were. Mostly kids come out and bother me. I don't get visitors much."

Carsten's heart slowly went back into its place, and he managed a wry smile. "I used to be one of those kids. But without the bothering. We tried to catch a glimpse of you."

"We?"

"Me and my three friends."

Mr. Jenkins came closer and took the print from him. "So you were one of those four, eh? I remember seein' you and wonderin' what you were doin'. Tryin' ta see me. If I'd known, I'd have made sure. Most kids did some kind of destruction instead."

Carsten smiled. "If you'd made an appearance, it probably would have scared us more than anythin'. We wanted to see you but also were scared to see you."

"Come. If you're not still scared of me, rest your horse a bit and come in for a cup o' coffee."

He took Sarai's reins and led her to the hitching post in front of his house and followed Mr. Jenkins into his cabin. For a bachelor's cabin, it was pretty tidy. Tidier than Carsten's would be if Ma wasn't there.

"What's your name, son?"

"Carsten Whitford." He sat down and waited for Mr. Jenkins to realize who he had invited in.

"Nice to meet you." The man went to the stove and poured two cups of coffee out of a pot. "Are you the son of that thief who went to prison?"

And there it was. Though different from most. "Yes."

"I knew the man had a son and always felt sorry for the boy. Growin' up without a father ain't easy." He came back to the table. "My pa died when I was twelve."

Carsten took a sip of coffee. "It's been hard, but Ma's been great. And Obadiah Raskins helps out when I need a man to talk to."

"Is that Raskins from the Bar X?"

"Yes, sir."

Mr. Jenkins shook his head. "I knew his pa. Good man."

"How much of the town news do you hear?"

"Not a lot." He leaned back on his chair. "When I get to town, Mr. Martin tries to make sure I know what is happening in town. Last I was in, he told me he got robbed. Some paper or somethin', but he seemed to make a big deal out of it."

"Did he say who he thought did it?"

"Some kid, but I don't think he said a name. Or he did and I don't remember. Why?"

Carsten shook his head. "No reason. Just curious." He finished his coffee slowly. Someone who didn't know what he'd done or even what he'd been accused of? He didn't think that was possible.

"What do you do when you aren't delivering prints?"

Carsten set his coffee cup aside. "I actually only started the deliveries a week ago. I have a farm and grow alfalfa for some of the ranchers in the area. What do you do?"

"I saved up quite a bit cowboyin' years ago, so now I live off that. Gives me a chance to be a crazy hermit. Every town needs one o' them anyhow. Scare the kids and generally be a creepy guy."

Carsten chuckled. "You succeeded in that. Although, now that I know you, you aren't scary."

"Thank you kindly."

Carsten stood and stretched. "Thanks for the coffee. I should get back home before Ma starts wondering where I disappeared to."

"Thanks for bringin' my print and for visiting with me. I've got an injury from the war in Mexico. It gave me some good stories, but I can't move as well anymore, and walkin' or ridin' to town is hard. I may be an old hermit, but I enjoy company once in a while."

"I was happy to do it. If you ever want to visit, feel free to stop by. I can't guarantee I'll be able to come out here much."

Mr. Jenkins shook his hand. "I appreciate it. Take care o' that ma of yours. She's a special lady."

Carsten mounted Sarai and rode off, only afterward wondering how Mr. Jenkins knew his ma. Maybe Ma could answer that question.

CHAPTER 12

Connections

When Carsten and his friends got together to discuss their plans, they decided Edmund and Carsten would go to town to try to figure out who could be part of the counterfeiting. It would be challenging since they had no idea what to look for or where to start.

Carsten walked on the right side of Edmund toward town. "Do we want to have a plan for when we get to town or wing it?" Carsten asked.

Edmund sighed. "I don't have any ideas for plans. Do you?"

"No. I think we should try to observe Mr. Graves and Carey Eldridge at the print shop." It was a smart move, even though he liked Mr. Graves and didn't think he was one of the crooks. "It would make sense for one or both to be part of it."

"Why?"

"What better place to print money than a print shop?"

Edmund grunted. "Good point. Mr. Graves seems like such a nice man, though. You really think he could be in on it?"

"I don't know. I have a sneaking suspicion which of them is more likely."

"Why?"

Carsten hesitated. "When I got the job delivering prints, I first fixed the press. Gobs of ink were stuck in the press, and Mr. Graves seemed genuinely surprised that it wasn't working. And he had no idea I was there until after he expressed his surprise."

"That does sound odd. When you helped Mrs. Eldridge, did you find anything that could be suspicious?"

"No, but Carey lives on his own now."

"Too bad. It would be nice to have some evidence."

Carsten let out a long breath. "We'll have to keep looking, and quickly."

"Has a date been set for the trial?"

They entered town, and Carsten scanned the road for the marshal. "No, not that I've been told anyway."

"You'd think the traveling judge would know when he'd be in town already. But I guess we won't have a deadline."

Carsten nodded. "A deadline would be nice, but we can only work with what we know."

"In the meantime, let's get this done."

They parted ways as they headed to the stores. Carsten stopped at the print shop first. It had been almost a week since he'd been there last.

"Mr. Graves?" Carsten stopped and let his eyes adjust to the dark room. Nobody. And no noise from the back. Odd. "Carey?" Carsten scrunched his eyebrows. "Anybody here?"

He went around the counter to the back and peeked past the open door. No one lay on the floor unconscious, but no one was in there either. Mr. Graves wouldn't leave his shop unattended and unlocked. Would he?

Thumping noises came from upstairs and then a grunt.

"Mr. Graves?" Carsten skirted the press and found the

stairs to the attic. They creaked all the way up as if it had been years since they'd been used. "Hello?"

"Carsten? Is that you?"

"Mr. Graves? Yes, it's me. What are you doing up here?" He finally reached the top of the stairs and looked into a dark, cobwebby room.

"Well," Mr. Graves said, "I got the notion to go through my trunk since it's so slow in the shop today, but it's heavier than I remember. Or I'm weaker." He laughed. "Not sure which."

"Can I help?"

"Would you?"

"I'm here and ventured up those creepy stairs. I may as well help you."

"Thanks, son." As Carsten made his way through the remaining cobwebs to him, Mr. Graves continued, "You know, I don't think the marshal got this one right. You wouldn't have stolen those papers. You'd have no use for them."

"That's kind of you to say." The papers. They'd be useful to a counterfeiter. Interesting.

"And you've done so many kind things for people."

They hefted the trunk and started toward the stairs.

"Mrs. Eldridge came in a few days ago to talk to her son, and he was busy, so we chatted for a bit. She said you fixed her house for her. I don't think a guilty man would be doing all these nice things. Do you?"

Carsten bit back a smirk. Mr. Graves was quite a talker. "No, I don't think so—"

"You've also maintained your innocence the whole way through," he interrupted. "Even a guilty man would be hard-pressed to do so under the same conditions."

They got the trunk to the top of the stairs and started down, with Carsten going first. "Pa did."

"Sure," Mr. Graves said, "but he was in jail at the time.

And he got caught red-handed. He didn't have much in the way of a defense. But you? I think there's plenty of people who will vouch for you. Especially Mrs. Eldridge."

"Thank you. I wish I could see that, but right now, I'm a bit discouraged. I don't know who would benefit from framing me for this. I mean, the real thief, of course, but who is it, and why did they steal the papers?"

"You're the only known thief in town. That's why. As for who would benefit, I don't know that answer."

Carsten hesitated. Would Mr. Graves help if he knew about the counterfeit money? No, it wasn't safe to confide in anyone else at this time.

They got safely to the bottom of the stairs, and Mr. Graves directed him to a corner of the back room. "It can go there. Now, what was that hesitation for?"

"What hesitation?"

"After I said I didn't know who would benefit from framing you."

Carsten's heart skipped a beat. "Well... We think we have an idea, sort of. But I don't think it's a good idea to share anything right now."

"Hm. If you need any help, let me know."

"Thanks. Where's Carey?"

"He asked for the day off and works so hard I told him to go ahead. Oh, and as for deliveries, there aren't any currently, but we'll have at least one by the end of the week. So come by either Friday or Saturday."

Carsten grinned. "You answered my question before I could ask it."

Mr. Graves chuckled. "Have a good day, and I'll be praying for your investigation. Have you talked to the marshal? Has he found the culprit?"

"Yep. Me. He's not looking anywhere else."

"Pshaw. I told the town council at the last meeting we should look into firing him, but no one else agreed."

"You're on the council?"

"Sure am."

It couldn't be that simple. Probably not, but Carsten had to ask. "Who else is part of the council?"

"Horace Comstock, me, Mayor Gion, and Theodore Baumgartner."

"What about the marshal?"

"He's an honorary member but not involved in the meetings. Why?"

Carsten shrugged. "Just curious. Thank you. You've given me a lot to think about. I'll see you Friday or Saturday."

Carsten rushed out before Mr. Graves could keep him longer. Carsten needed to find Edmund and go over his thoughts. Edmund was leaving the General Store when Carsten exited the print shop. They met halfway, and Carsten dragged Edmund down the alley between the stores.

"What? Where are we going?"

"Somewhere we can't be overheard," Carsten whispered.

"Why?"

Carsten took a deep breath. "Mr. Graves said something interesting that made me wonder. He thinks the marshal needs to be replaced, but no one else on the town council agrees. What if some of the council are involved in the counterfeiting?"

"How did you come up with that?"

"Mr. Graves." Carsten summarized his conversation about the council.

"Hm." Edmund frowned. "What would any of them have to gain?"

"Making the town seem more prosperous than its neighbors in any direction."

Edmund sucked in a whistling breath. "That might make sense."

Carsten leaned against a wall. They had a new idea, but what could they do about it? Keep doing what they came to town for. "We should get back out there and try to observe some of these people."

"Okay. I'll watch the marshal, if I can, and maybe try to spot the mayor. I think you should try to talk to Mr. Baumgartner."

"I need to talk to him anyway, so that works well."

"Let's meet at the café when you're done at the feed store."

Carsten laughed.

"What?"

"I think it's interesting. I call it the seed store, but you call it the feed store."

"Heh. Well, that makes sense."

"See you at the café."

Carsten headed to Baumgartner's store. He was busy, so Carsten looked around while trying to casually observe the owner. There were two men and one woman, who looked bored to death, inside. There were so many different types of feed. Not as many seeds, but keeping them in stock unused was not a good idea. Carsten glanced at Mr. Baumgartner as he talked to one of the other farmers. What did a counterfeiter look like? Did they give off any clues? Carsten shuddered. If they got caught looking into him and he ended up being a counterfeiter, he would be a dangerous opponent. Theodore Baumgartner was one of the tallest and burliest men in town. No one, not even gunslingers, dared cross him.

"What can I do for you, Carsten?" Mr. Baumgartner's voice boomed across the store.

Carsten had gotten lost in thought. Again. He cleared his throat. "I'm wondering if you have any new varieties of alfalfa mix. I have a customer who wants to try something new if I can afford it for my next crop."

"Come up here, and I'll grab the catalog." Mr. Baumgartner turned around as Carsten took the last two steps to the counter. "I assume you want it to be about the same price as the alfalfa you have bought in the past."

"Yes." Carsten looked around as he reached the counter. He didn't see anything that would be incriminating to him, but Mr. Baumgartner was a smart man, not the type to leave things out.

"Ah. Here it is." The owner faced Carsten and handed the catalog to him. "There's a few new types of alfalfa under the *a*'s. I haven't looked at them yet so don't know the prices. Would you be ordering it today or just looking?"

"Just looking."

"Smart idea. You can order it after the trial, if you are innocent."

"Mm-hm." The man's words didn't register right away. When they did, Carsten looked up. "I am innocent."

"'Course." Mr. Baumgartner snorted. "All criminals say so until the judge says otherwise."

Carsten wanted to say something but decided not to. Mr. Baumgartner's mind was made up. Carsten wouldn't be able to change it. Not unless he was able to prove someone else stole the papers. He browsed the descriptions. The one that seemed most similar to what Obadiah was looking for was also quite a bit more expensive. Which meant Carsten could charge more for it, but he wouldn't be able to pay for the seeds. He sighed.

"Find what you want?"

"Yeah, but I can't afford it."

"Maybe your customer would pay you some before he gets the product."

"I can ask, but that's not how I prefer to do things."

"I could extend you some credit but probably not enough for what you want."

Why would he offer Carsten credit? No one offered him credit. "I don't want to owe anyone. I don't take credit for that reason."

Mr. Baumgartner gave a slight smile. "Well, let me know if you decide to get it anyway, and I'll order it for you."

"Thanks."

"Anything else I can do for you?"

Tell me if you're involved in the counterfeiting. Carsten forced himself to smile. "No, I don't think so."

"I'll talk to you later."

Carsten headed out of the store and to the café. As he did, he saw the marshal and paused. Did he pass him or...

The marshal approached and stopped near Carsten. "Stay out of trouble," the marshal hissed.

Carsten's nostrils flared, and something on the marshal's hands caught his attention. He stared, almost too long, at them. A red stain on the marshal's hands. Blood? No, he wouldn't be that evil. Carsten's steps faltered as he walked past the marshal without answering. Fragments of thoughts worked together in his mind. Red ink caked in the printing press. A red stain on the marshal's hands. The convenience of a known former thief accused of stealing fancy paper from the General Store.

Could it be that simple? Carsten entered the café and went straight to the table where Edmund sat and pulled out the five-dollar bill in his pocket. A cream paper with a red seal. He sucked in a breath and laid the money in front of Edmund.

CHAPTER 13
Hooked

Two weeks had passed since meeting Amelia and Emmeline. Lonzo had done little on the job besides paperwork, which he knew more thoroughly than he thought possible. Captain Bertram had made sure of that. Lonzo read every report that came in and now knew that the style didn't matter as long as every important detail was in there.

It wasn't normal to follow up, but Captain Bertram let him do so with Amelia and Emmeline. Lonzo went to the mansion and found that they were doing well. Their father, Mr. Wilson, had started helping clean and fix things up as well as find reliable servants.

Lonzo knew he wouldn't always be able to see a job through to its conclusion, but he was thankful his first one was close to home. Or office anyway.

But today, Lonzo guessed things were going to change. He stepped into the dark office and waited for his eyes to adjust.

"Mornin', Priscilla. How's the family?"

The woman laughed. "Same as yesterday, Lonzo. Asking every day isn't going to change the answer. The children are at school and doing well. My husband is still working the same job he's had for years."

Lonzo chuckled. "Yes, ma'am. Glad things are doing well. Boss man in?"

"Of course."

Lonzo leaned on Priscilla's desk. "Tell me. Does he ever go home?"

"Not often."

"Has he ever married?"

"Why all the questions?" Priscilla asked.

"He never answers them. I figure you know enough about him after working here so long."

"How long do you think I have worked for him?"

Lonzo shrugged. "Longer than I have."

Priscilla scowled. "Naturally. As far as I know, he has never married. Now, get into the boss man's office before he comes out to find you cavorting with the secret'ry."

Lonzo stood and saluted. "Yes, ma'am." He knocked on the office door before opening it. "Mornin', Captain. What's the job today?"

"Come in and close the door," Captain Bertram said.

Lonzo did so and sat down. "You look serious."

"I am. We've learned of a kidnapping. It happened two days ago near Fort Worth. I need you to go with Zachariah and find the child."

"Yes, sir. Where is Zachariah, and when do we leave?"

"Go home and pack your bags. Zachariah will meet you here in thirty minutes."

"Yes, sir." Heart pounding, Lonzo headed out the door, barely registering Priscilla's farewell. Who would kidnap a child? And why? He hurried home, packed his saddlebags, and saddled his horse. Food. He had some bread that would survive the trip. Hopefully they could get more food in Fort Worth. After stuffing the bread into a saddlebag, he swung up onto the saddle and trotted down to the Rangers' office.

A large man stood next to a black horse. "Lonzo?"

"Yes. You must be Zachariah?"

"I am. I got permission to leave for Fort Worth. I know a few more details than you and will brief you on the way."

"Yes, sir." Lonzo followed Zachariah out of town and then moved next to him to get the details.

"The child walked home from school as usual but never arrived home. A couple friends saw him a few houses from his home. Then he disappeared. No one knows where he went."

"But they think he was kidnapped rather than running away?"

"Yes. His books were found scattered on the ground. He was a tidy young man who apparently wouldn't want his books getting dirty."

"I see." Lonzo scratched his chin. "I assume someone talked to the neighbors."

Zachariah sighed. "Yes."

"Sorry for all the questions. This is my first kidnapping case."

Zachariah shifted on his saddle. "From what I'm told, it's your first case besides being chaperone."

"True. I look forward to learning from you."

"Good. Then you know you need to observe for a while."

"Yes, sir." Lonzo concentrated on what Zachariah told him about the case, repeating some of the more important details so he wouldn't forget them.

THEY RODE into Fort Worth early the next day, questioned people about the child, and searched. Nothing turned up, and they needed to find a lead. Lonzo knew he wasn't supposed to go out on his own, but he woke up early the second morning and spent some time reading the Bible and praying, especially about the missing boy. During his prayer, inspiration hit him, and he left his room, then slid a note under Zachariah's door.

He left his Ranger star in his pocket and walked out to the area where the boy had disappeared. Most of the buildings were occupied, but a couple appeared abandoned. Lonzo closed his eyes, imagining where the shadows would be in the afternoon. The alley. That would be the perfect place for the kidnapper to hide. A boy wouldn't suspect anything. He passed the alley hundreds of times. The kidnapper snatched him, scattering the books, covering the boy's mouth and…

Lonzo opened his eyes and went down the alley, searching every little dust speck and stain on the walls and ground. Nothing there. Not yet. He kept going and made it to the end of the alley. Which way would the kidnapper have gone? Toward the boy's home or away? Lonzo glanced in both directions before something to the left caught his eye.

Another book.

The boy at least had the presence of mind to keep one book and toss it when he could. Smart kid. Hopefully his intelligence would keep him alive. Lonzo walked down the back alley to the next street. Shops lined this street and would be busy in the afternoons, especially after school. A kidnapper wouldn't be able to drag a boy here. Which meant they probably would have taken him into one of the houses or buildings Lonzo had already passed.

Lonzo saw a tuft of grass, bent down, and pulled a long blade of grass, sticking it in his mouth to chew on while he thought. He headed back the way he came, examining each doorway and window. If he was a kidnapper, where would he stash a kid—whether permanently or for a few hours?

A broken window. So this building was likely unoccupied. He needed help. Lonzo made a mental note and headed back to the hotel. He made it halfway before seeing Zachariah's tall form coming at him.

"You left without me."

"Uh-huh. But I found something, and I have an idea. Got your gun on you?"

Zachariah scoffed. "Always."

"Good. We might need it."

Zachariah raised an eyebrow. "Want to tell me what's up?"

"I found another schoolbook in an alley. The alley leads out to a busy street. The boy could have been put in an abandoned building until dark. If we're lucky, he'll still be there."

"And if we aren't?"

"We at least have a little more information than we did before. This kid's smart. He left a book behind, I think on purpose, so he might have left us a clue in the building. If he's not there."

"Let's search the building."

Lonzo led him to the building, and they entered, guns ready to draw at a second's notice. They took different sides and stepped over broken furniture and piles of dirt. Lonzo found nothing as he reached the center of the back of the room with Zachariah.

"Empty," Zachariah whispered. "Let's go upstairs."

Lonzo nodded and led the way up the stairs. The second step creaked, and Lonzo winced, then stopped. The floor upstairs creaked, and a shoe hit the floor. They were no longer sneaking up anyway, so Lonzo raced up the rickety steps and burst onto the second floor. Someone stood over a boy, gun pointed at him. The kidnapper had a hat hiding his face, and the boy hid the rest of him.

Lonzo's breath stopped. "Hey, you don't need to point the gun at the kid." He motioned for Zachariah to stay downstairs. "I want to get the boy safely home to his parents."

"Stay back." The high-pitched voice hesitated. "I'll... I'll shoot him if I have to."

Lonzo's heart skipped a beat. The kidnapper was a woman. That was a feminine voice. Her hands shook. She didn't want to kill the kid. She hadn't hurt him, from what

Lonzo could see. The boy had tear-stained cheeks, wide, red eyes, and a quivering lip, but there was no blood. Yet. Talking someone out of shooting a kid was not on Lonzo's list of things he had ever wanted to deal with. *God, help me.*

Lonzo shuffled one step closer. "Can you stop pointing the gun at Mikey?"

"His name's William," the woman said. She refused to look away from the boy she held close to her side.

"Okay, what's your name?"

"Wilhelmina."

"That's a pretty name. Do you have a husband? I see a ring on your finger."

"No, he died a week ago."

"I'm sorry, Wilhelmina. Did you have any children?"

"Just William here."

Lonzo glanced down at Zachariah. Zachariah gave him a nod and backed down the stairs. This was a start. "How old is William?"

"Ten."

"Wilhelmina, this boy in front of you is only eight. He isn't your son. Isn't that right, Mikey?"

"I'm Mikey, and I'm eight. My family is waiting for me at home. I have a dad, mom, and two sisters. One older and one younger."

"No. You're my son, William. I can't let you go yet. You left me too soon."

Lonzo shuffled forward a little bit. "Wilhelmina, I'm so sorry for your loss. I know it is really hard to lose a loved one. My father died three years ago. I had a hard time letting him go, too. A boy needs his father. Is that why William and your husband were together last week?"

"Yes. They went fishing together. I knew something was wrong when they didn't come home for lunch. But I waited until supper before talking to the sheriff. What if I'd said something sooner? Could I have saved them?"

"You can't torture yourself with those questions, ma'am. You have no idea if they would be alive if you said something sooner. Please let the boy go home to his parents. I'll stay here and talk with you as long as you need me to."

She looked at Lonzo for the first time. "You would do that?"

"Yes. Let Mikey go home."

Wilhelmina dropped the gun and let go of the boy, then buried her head in her hands, sobbing.

Mikey ran into Lonzo's arms as soon as the woman let go, and Lonzo held him close. "You are a brave boy," he whispered. "Go down the stairs. My Ranger friend Zachariah should be down there."

Mikey let out a shuddering breath. "Okay. Thank you."

"You're welcome. Now go." Lonzo let go of him, and Mikey rushed down the stairs. Lonzo knelt and slowly moved closer to Wilhelmina. Once he got close enough, he took her gun and moved it out of reach. "What was your husband's name?"

"Milo."

"A good, strong name. What did he do for work?"

"Ranch hand."

"That mean you lived out on a ranch?"

"No, a small farm near it."

Lonzo chuckled. "So you got to work in the dirt with the farmin'?"

Wilhelmina looked up. "Yes."

"You liked it."

She smiled.

Lonzo held a hand out to Wilhelmina. "My ma always loved the gardening and weeding. Not so much the canning, though. She always said it didn't make sense why you needed to preserve all that food in the hottest months of the year. But my sisters loved canning, so it worked out once they were old enough to take over."

"Your ma and I would get along well." Wilhelmina looked down and wrung her hands. "How did she get over the death of her husband?"

"Lots of prayer and patience."

Wilhelmina forced a laugh. "I don't have much of either."

"You could. I'm sure there's a pastor and his wife here who could help you."

"I'm not much of a church person. I never really went before and don't think I should now."

"Why?"

Wilhelmina shrugged. "Goin' out of desperation isn't exactly the smartest thing to do."

"When else are you gonna go? I go to God out of desperation all the time. I prayed to Him out of desperation when I saw you up here with Mikey. I didn't know what to say to you. All those words that came out of my mouth? Those were His, not mine."

"Really?"

Lonzo put a hand on her shoulder. "Really. You will probably have to go to jail for a while, though. At least until the judge makes a decision on what to do. But I'll talk to a pastor about coming to visit you there to talk to you."

Wilhelmina exhaled slowly. "I didn't hurt that boy, did I?"

"I'm sure he'll be fine."

"Good. I want to talk to someone if they can come to the jail."

Lonzo stood and helped Wilhelmina up. "I'll make sure they do."

"You're a good man. What is your name?"

"Lonzo Hossman."

"Lonzo. That's an unusual name."

"Yes, it is. My pa heard it somewhere and loved it. After four girls, Ma told him if they had a boy, he could name him."

Wilhelmina laughed and followed him down the stairs. "When did you become a Ranger?"

"Two weeks ago."

Wilhelmina stopped at the bottom of the steps. "Wouldn't be able to tell you're a new Ranger by the way you handled me. Couldn't have been easy."

"No, but like I said…"

"God helped ya."

"Exactly," Lonzo said.

They left the building and found Zachariah leaning against the doorframe.

"Ma'am, did this young Ranger charm you into comin' down to the jail?"

Wilhelmina let out a breath. "It was a bit of charm and persuasion combined. Whoever trained him did a good job."

"'Fraid I can't take credit," Zachariah said. "This is my first job with him. Lonzo, you can take a break now. I'll get Wilhelmina to the sheriff's office."

"Thanks. I'm going to check in on Mikey."

"Don't get too attached to the kid. Getting too attached to a client never ends well."

Zachariah left with Wilhelmina, and Lonzo headed down the street to Mikey's house, where he knocked on the door.

A man opened the door. "Can I help you?"

"My name is Lonzo. I helped find Mikey. I wanted to see how he's doing."

The man engulfed him in a tight hug. "Thank you for bringing our boy back to us. The other Ranger said you're the one who talked to the kidnapper and saved him. Come in. The doctor is making sure everything is all right."

Lonzo removed himself from the father's grasp and followed him into the small house. Mikey sat on a chair with a doctor poking and prodding him.

"That's him!" Mikey exclaimed. "That's the Ranger who saved me from that woman."

"Sit still for a couple more minutes," the doctor said.

"Sorry," Mikey said.

Lonzo crouched near Mikey. "Did she hurt you anywhere?"

"No. I was scared more than anything. I didn't think she would let me go."

"I'm glad you're all right," Lonzo said. "You are all busy and wanting to spend some time alone, so I'll go. I wanted to make sure everything was all right. I'm sure the sheriff will want to talk to all three of you about Wilhelmina, but he can wait until tomorrow, if you would prefer."

"Thank you," Mikey's pa said. "For everything."

"We were happy to help."

Lonzo let himself out the front door and went back to the sheriff's office. Zachariah was just leaving.

"You did good, Lonzo." Zachariah slapped Lonzo's back. "And it's early enough we could go back if you're ready."

Lonzo grinned. "All I need to do is get my bag out of the hotel. Just like you."

Zachariah grinned back. "Then let's go."

CHAPTER 14
Rushed

E dmund stared at the five and then at Carsten with a raised eyebrow. "What's this for?"

Carsten whispered, "Red ink. That's the connection. Someone at the print shop is involved. The press had red ink caked in it, which made it stop working. I just saw the marshal, and he has a red stain on his hands. The marshal and someone at the print shop have to be part of this."

Edmund leaned back, eyes wide, but didn't say anything as the waitress approached.

"Can I get you anything, Carsten?" she asked.

Carsten's mind went blank. "Just water, please. Oh, and a slice of apple pie." He waited until she left. "Well?"

"Is there any other reason the marshal could have red ink on him?"

"He could have made it, I suppose. But red isn't a color most people write with."

"Why wouldn't the marshal try to wash it off?"

"It's hard to wash ink off. I got some on my hands when I helped Mr. Graves fix his press, and it's still there but fainter, even with me scrubbing it hard with Ma's soap."

Edmund took a drink of his coffee. "Although, if he got

107

the ink on his hands when you did, you wouldn't have seen it this time."

"He could've worked with the press since then. They would have learned from the last time it got clogged up."

"And he actually works with the ink? He doesn't have enough people to pawn it off to?" Edmund huffed. "Well, it's a good place to start. We need to figure out who else could be part of it. If there's anyone. You're sure Mr. Graves isn't involved?"

"Pretty sure. I don't see how he could have acted so clue-less about the press getting clogged. And he's been using the press so long he would have figured out what was wrong if he'd known what it was used for."

"So it must be Carey Eldridge, then."

They paused as the waitress approached.

"Here's your pie," she said. "And your water. Can I get either of you anything else?"

"Thank you, no," Edmund said.

"No, thank you." Carsten took a bite of the apple pie. Not quite as good as Ma's but definitely tasty. "Could they be doing it together—just the two of them? Or do they have help?"

"I'm not sure. It would be easier to figure out if we knew what their reasons were for doing it. Is it to get rich? To make the town seem richer than it is? Settle debts?"

"I know." Carsten sighed. "Carey Eldridge has always been poor, like me. But the marshal? He might have vices we know nothing about."

"And are any of the councilmen involved somehow?"

"We should talk to someone who knows them better," Carsten said.

"I could talk to Luella, if you want."

"No, I want to see if she'll talk to me anyway. Who would know Mr. Baumgartner?"

"Not sure. We can't tell anyone what our suspicions are,

so how do we ask people without telling them what we're looking for?"

Carsten sighed and took a few more bites of his pie before speaking again. "With Luella, I could try to find out if her pa has any money troubles." He snorted. "That might be weird, too."

"Let's not worry about it anymore today. We can talk to Amos and Kit tomorrow. Maybe one of them will have an idea."

"Maybe." Carsten dug into his pie and finished it. He could feel Edmund's eyes on him but chose to keep from looking up.

"Anything else? Or should we go back home now?"

Carsten wasn't sure how to answer that. He wanted to go home. Get away from all of this intrigue. But he also wanted to stay. Talk to Luella and get to the bottom of this counterfeiting. What conflicted his heart so much? "I don't know. I don't think there is much else we can do here. Or there is, and I haven't thought of it."

"Then let's go home, and we'll figure it out tomorrow with Amos and Kit." Edmund stood and set some money on the table.

Carsten hesitated before standing. "Okay."

They walked out into the sunlit day. He blinked at the sudden brightness. As his eyes adjusted, a flash of metal caught his attention. Marshal Lydick was back to watching him again. Carsten needed to go home. He also wanted to know how long they had. "I'm gonna talk to the marshal about when the trial is. I'll go home after."

"You sure you don't want me to stay?"

"Yes."

Edmund kept his eyes on Carsten for a while. "Okay. See you tomorrow."

Carsten waited until his friend was out of sight before turning to confront the marshal. But he wasn't there. He had disappeared. Carsten narrowed his eyes and headed for the marshal's office. When he reached it, a man he knew was coming out.

"Mr. Comstock!" Carsten said.

The man kept walking.

"Mr. Comstock? How is Luella?"

Mr. Comstock kept moving away from him, and Carsten stood there, dumbfounded. What was up with that? Mr. Comstock had never completely ignored him before. So what had changed? Why did Luella's family suddenly start avoiding Carsten?

Carsten let out a long breath and turned back to the marshal's office. What would Mr. Comstock talk to the marshal about? He wasn't involved, was he? No. He wouldn't do that to Luella and her mother. Would he?

Carsten's heart sank into his stomach. Was that why Luella didn't talk to him? Was her pa involved and trying to poison her against Carsten?

Carsten spun around and walked quickly to the Comstocks' home. He had to talk to Luella. He had to see if she knew anything. When he got to the house, she was outside weeding the flower garden, humming one of the hymns from church.

He approached slowly and cleared his throat. "Luella, can we talk? For a few minutes?"

She didn't look at him. "You have until I finish weeding."

Carsten let out a breath. "How are you doing?"

"Fine."

"And your parents?"

"They're fine."

"Good. What's your pa up to these days?"

"Always the same. He leaves at seven in the morning to go to work and comes back before dinner."

"Has he left after dinner at all?"

Luella shrugged. "I don't think so. Why?"

"Just wondering."

Luella finally looked up at him. "Shouldn't you be trying to find the person who did the robbery? Not questioning me about Papa?"

"I would, but…" He hesitated. "There's more to this."

"Like what?"

"I can't tell you."

She stood and put her hands on her hips. "Why not, and what does that have to do with Papa?"

"It's complicated."

"How?"

Carsten sat on the porch step. "We found out about something else going on and think it's related to the robbery. I don't even know for sure if your pa is involved."

"No. Absolutely not." Luella scoffed. "Papa wouldn't be part of anything bad." Her hand trembled as she pointed toward the road. "You need to go. Now."

"Luella."

"Go."

Carsten stood and pursed his lips. "I'm sorry. I sincerely hope I am wrong."

"You are. Go back home now."

"I'm going." Carsten walked home in a daze. He'd hurt Luella. She believed in her pa. And she had every right to. He had believed in his pa, too, until his pa had been caught.

He really hoped Mr. Comstock wasn't involved in the counterfeiting. Of everybody in town, Carsten was the only one who knew what it was like to have a pa as a criminal. He didn't want Luella to have to go through that.

CHAPTER 15

Injury

"They have to be making the counterfeit money at night." Carsten stood facing his friends, who sat at his ma's table. "That's when the press broke down. It's the only time they could get away with it."

Edmund nodded. "You're right. We need to go to town around midnight if we want to find out who is involved."

"I…" Carsten's stomach clenched. "I'm not sure if that's a smart idea. It's too dangerous. I can't let you three risk getting hurt. If we're caught, they could injure us."

"You think you should go alone?" Amos grunted. "To a town that already thinks you're a thief? In the dark? No. That's not happening. We're coming with you, and you won't fight us on that. We'll go tonight."

Kit took a light breath. "Let's meet by the magnolia tree at dark. From there, we can figure out exactly where in town we want to hide out so we can see both doors."

"I really don't think it's a good idea," Carsten said. "It could be dangerous."

"We'll take that risk," Amos said. "This is the one thing you really can't do alone."

"I know. But…"

"Don't give it another thought," Kit said. "We may as well all get in trouble, not just you."

Carsten chuckled. "What a way to put it. Well, I guess it can't go too badly. I'll see you guys tonight. Did you want to stay for supper? I'm sure Ma would be fine with it."

"Pa and Ma don't know about me staying for dinner, though," Amos said.

Kit tapped his foot. "True. But I think they'll figure it out and won't mind. Unless there's some reason your parents would have for not trusting you."

Edmund laughed. "Mine don't. I think it's a good idea."

"You're sure your ma won't mind, Carsten?" Amos asked.

"When have I ever minded you boys staying over for a meal or overnight?" Ma asked as she walked into the house.

Amos ducked his head. "Never. But it doesn't hurt to ask."

"Before I decide for sure, though," Ma said, "what're you boys up to?"

Carsten went over and put a hand on Ma's shoulder. "We're going to town to observe any late-night activities."

Ma pursed her lips. "Is that wise?"

"We'll be careful," Carsten assured her.

"You better be. I don't want to lose any of you." She straightened. "I've got three extra mouths to feed, so I need to start on dinner. While I do, you boys go out of the house and do something."

"Yes, ma'am!" they said in unison.

AFTER DINNER, they snoozed in Carsten's loft until the clock struck nine. Before dozing off, they'd decided to split into groups of two. One group would stay near the marshal's office, and the other near the print shop. Then they would observe and follow as needed.

"You guys ready?" Carsten whispered as the last light faded over the horizon.

"Huh?" Edmund grunted. "Yeah, let's get to town before the counterfeiters disappear with all their loot."

"Edmund." Kit groaned.

"I'm kidding! Let's go."

They climbed down the ladder and quietly opened the door.

"I need to wake up some," Kit said as they stepped out into the chilly outdoors. "Anyone want to race to the magnolia tree?"

"You're on!" Amos exclaimed.

Edmund and Carsten looked at each other and shrugged. "May as well," Edmund said.

They lined up, and Carsten counted off. He didn't try to go fast to start. When running, he preferred to pace himself, so he would start slow, then speed up as he got closer to his goal.

Amos started out in the lead, with Edmund not too far behind. Kit seemed to pace himself as well.

By the time the tree was in sight, they were all neck and neck. Carsten sped up on the last stretch and beat his friends to the tree by mere inches and collapsed under it. "Phew! That was fun."

Kit laughed. "Yes. Yes it was. But now I'm more exhausted in a different way. Whose idea was this?"

Amos socked him on the shoulder. "Yours."

Kit groaned. "Worst idea possible. How am I supposed to hide quietly when all my muscles are crying out for mercy?"

"You wanna go home?" Edmund asked.

"'Course not! I'm tryin' to be funny."

Carsten shook his head. "It's not working. Speaking of working, we should get the rest of the way into town."

"Yep," Amos agreed. "Edmund and I will be by the print shop. Good luck keeping Kit quiet, Carsten."

"Thanks," Carsten answered. "I'll do my best."

"You'd better, or the marshal'll catch you." Edmund winked. "See ya 'round town."

Kit and Carsten hung back until the other two disappeared into the darkness. "Ready?"

"As I'll ever be," Kit said. "You sure you want to take the marshal's office? Might be safer for you at the print shop."

"Too late to switch now. And I don't mind."

"Good. Time to go."

They walked into town and went to the alley next to the post office and across from the marshal's office. They found a spot in some shadows to keep an eye on things. Carsten had hoped they could be right next to the building, but the light streaming from the window in the marshal's office made it too bright over there. The residual light from the marshal's office made it so they could even see the print shop from where they crouched.

"You okay?" Carsten whispered to Kit.

"Yes. Why wouldn't I be?"

"Your sore muscles."

Kit snorted. "Hilarious. I'm fine. I don't have sore muscles."

Carsten smiled. "Just trying to pass the time."

"Great. We'll get caught for sure if you keep yammering."

Carsten decided not to respond. As the minutes ticked by, his mind wandered to Luella. He wondered how she was doing after their conversation. It had been so stupid to talk to her about her pa. At least the way he had. He wanted to catch the person who set him up, not hurt people or make them think badly of him or other people. Unless the people were the actual thief. Then he didn't care how they were thought of.

Carsten sincerely hoped Mr. Comstock wasn't involved in the counterfeiting. He seemed to do well for himself, so needing money couldn't be a reason. What other reason would there be? Greed, maybe. But that didn't seem Mr. Comstock's style.

Movement caught his eye. Someone stumbled out of one of the bars across the street and down the road past the print shop and marshal's office. False alarm.

Kit sighed. "This could be a long, boring night."

"Maybe. We'll have to wait and see. Wait. Who's that?" Carsten pointed across the street.

"In the marshal's office? Not the marshal unless he's changed his look to be more feminine."

"And grew his hair out?" Carsten asked. "I don't think so. Maybe it's his sweetheart. I know he mentioned one when I was in the jail."

"Ugh!" Kit exclaimed in disgust. "I hope she is. He's kissing her!"

Carsten shuddered. "Is it really that bad that he likes his girl?"

"No, but in public?"

"He's behind a closed door. They shouldn't be in front of a window, but they're both grown adults. And no one is out this late at night. It's not exactly public."

Kit shrugged. "I suppose. It's still a bit shocking. Think she's in on it?"

"Probably not. Most women enjoy gossiping. Or at least that's what they say."

"So the marshal wouldn't trust her. Too bad. We could have tried to talk her into telling us more about it."

"I don't think that's a good idea. Turning sweethearts or wives against their men isn't as effective in this type of thing."

"Maybe not, but it could be helpful if the ladies would talk."

"Now who's yammering?"

Kit chuckled softly. "Sorry."

They lapsed into silence again. Carsten glanced at the

marshal's window. The kissing couple had moved. When had his girl gotten into the office? Must have been before they got there. A few minutes later, the marshal's office door opened, and she came out.

"There she goes. Wanna question her?" Carsten asked.

"Har-har. No, thanks."

"Good. I'd have talked you out of it."

"Stop trying to make me laugh," Kit said. "I'm not supposed to be making noise."

"Sorry. I'll try to stop talking."

"Thanks."

They watched without talking for a while again. Carsten had never stayed in one place long in town. Now he was glad he hadn't. The smells of stale beer, human waste, and perfume were overwhelming in this alley. Nothing at all like the smells of the wide-open spaces on the farms and ranches out of town. Of course, there you usually had the scents of manure, but he could live with that better.

Something moved in the marshal's office.

Carsten squinted. "Is that the marshal in the office?"

"I was wondering the same thing. I don't think so."

"Who is it?"

Kit hesitated. "I'm... I'm not sure. He is bigger than the marshal. Maybe it's Mr. Baumgartner?"

"Perhaps. I don't know. Should we go in for a closer look?"

"Does it matter? Even if it is him, we don't know why he's there. Could be a law enforcement reason."

Carsten grunted. "Yeah. Why are we here again?"

Kit put a hand on his shoulder. "To try to find a way to prove your innocence or find out who is counterfeiting."

"I know. Should we go find Edmund and Amos? See if they've noticed anything?"

"Wait." Kit's hand tightened on Carsten's shoulder. "Look."

"What is it?"

"The marshal's office. Someone new is coming out."

Kit and Carsten leaned forward as the marshal and mystery man left the office and headed down toward the print shop. They stopped in front of the store next to the print shop. They talked for a few minutes, then took a few more steps toward the print shop. They stepped into the alley, and Kit and Carsten lost sight of them.

The back door.

Of course they would use the back door instead of the front. Would Amos and Edmund have thought of that? Were they able to see?

"We need to go over there," Carsten said.

Kit followed Carsten. No one loitered in the streets, so they sprinted across and crept down the boardwalk in the shadows toward the alley where the marshal and his friend disappeared. At the alley, Carsten peeked in. The moon didn't give off enough light for him to see anything. They would have to take a chance. Unless…

Carsten turned to Kit. "Let's get behind the print shop."

"Why?" Kit whispered back.

"So we don't accidentally run into the marshal and his friend."

A hand hit Carsten, and he started, his heart nearly jumping out of his chest.

"Hiya," Amos whispered. "The marshal and his friend went into the print shop. In case you wondered."

"We did," Kit said. "Now what?"

"Let's go back there," Carsten suggested, "and wait to see who he's with."

"There's not enough light, and the moon will be setting soon," Edmund said.

"We need to decide in case they come out," Carsten said. "I think we should go behind the church. It will be dark there, we can hide, and it's close enough so we can see them. If we can't see faces, fine. We'll figure out what to do then. If we can, then we figure out who to talk to about it and tell the authorities."

Edmund sighed. "He's right. This is why we're here." He started toward the church on the other side of the print shop, and the rest of the boys followed.

They reached the back of the church and huddled in the shadows. Time passed slowly. Carsten tried to keep himself from talking this time. Amos didn't. He always chatted when he was nervous, though, so Carsten wasn't surprised.

The print shop's door opened, letting light into the alley, and Carsten tapped Amos's shoulder. The latter quit talking, and all four young men watched as Carey Eldridge stepped outside and looked around the back alley. Another man came out after him but never looked toward the church, so they couldn't see who it was.

Carsten took low, shallow breaths, trying to keep himself from moving and giving them away. He could hear the breath from his three friends as well and hoped it didn't carry down the alley.

A sneeze behind him made Carsten and the two people behind the print shop look. Kit immediately apologized, but it was too late.

Carey and his friend ran back into the print shop. Carsten turned around and stared at his friends, eyes wide and heart pounding. They went around the church to the front. They were almost out of town when three masked men came at them with sticks or something. Carsten and his friends tried to fend them off, but they were smaller than the three armed men.

Carsten lost track of his friends as he fended off his attacker. The man was big and sweaty. All Carsten's efforts to get away or hurt the guy were in vain. He got a few blows in, but the attacker hit his left shoulder with the club, sending shooting pain through it and down Carsten's arm. His ears buzzed and vision blurred, and he fell to the ground. The next blow hit his ribs, and Carsten struggled to catch his breath. He kicked out at the attacker's legs and somehow managed to knock him down. Carsten caught his breath long enough to stand up and start running. As he ran, he glanced around and saw each of his three friends running as well. They left their attackers in the dust.

CHAPTER 16

Help

W hen they reached the magnolia tree, Carsten stopped. "I need a rest. I..." He winced and a low groan escaped. "My ribs took a beating, and I'm having a hard time breathing. I think they wanted to scare us, and they succeeded."

"Doesn't look as if they're following us," Amos said. "How badly hurt are you all?"

"Just a few bruises," Edmund said.

Kit took his left hand off his right arm. "I got a pretty good cut, but otherwise, I'm good."

"I'm okay, too," Amos said. "He got a blow on my head, but I've got a thick skull. Carsten?"

"Something's not right with my shoulder. It got hit hard and hurts more than my ribs."

Amos came over and touched Carsten's left shoulder. Pain radiated through it, and Carsten let out an involuntary groan.

"Let's go to my ranch. Pa'll know what to do better than your ma."

Carsten nodded. "Okay. Lead the way." He held his arm against his stomach and took a few steps.

"You gonna make it?" Kit asked.

"Yeah. Let's get there before I pass out."

Carsten kept his eyes on the friend in front of him. Running had been fine because he hadn't felt the pain yet. But after the break, the pain gradually got worse until he couldn't stop thinking about it. He tried to keep his mind anywhere but on the excruciating pain. Not an easy feat. Fire shot straight through his shoulder and into his arm and left side. Walking jostled it, even though he tried not to let it.

By the time they stumbled into the Bar X's ranch house, his vision had narrowed. He sat on the nearest chair and tried to keep his shoulder completely still. As he sat there, he prayed silently. *God, we need more help. I don't know who, but we need someone else to finish this investigation. Help us, please!*

"Carsten." Obadiah's voice sounded far away, but he was touching Carsten's bad arm.

Carsten took a deep breath and winced at the pain it caused.

"Carsten," Obadiah continued, "I need you to stay awake for me. Open your eyes."

They were closed? Carsten used his last effort to pry them open.

"There you go. Now, Amos said your shoulder hurts. What happened to it?"

"Someone hit it hard with a club," Carsten ground out.

"Okay. I'm going to have to touch it to see if I can feel any damage."

Carsten gave a quick nod and took in a slow, deep breath.

Obadiah poked and prodded Carsten's shoulder for a few seconds. "It's dislocated. I need to pop it back in place. It won't be pleasant, but you should have almost immediate relief."

Carsten didn't have a chance to reply before he was moved onto his back on the floor with a hand holding his.

"All right," Obadiah said as he put a foot on Carsten's shoulder gently. "One, two."

Carsten's shoulder exploded in even more pain, and his vision went dark. The next thing he knew, he was lying on the settee in the parlor, and his three friends were there chatting with Obadiah.

Carsten sat up slowly with a light groan. His shoulder still hurt, but it was an ache rather than burning fire.

"You're awake!" Edmund exclaimed. "Told ya he'd be fine."

"Fine?" Carsten questioned. "Not sure that's the word I'd use."

"How's the shoulder?" Obadiah asked.

"Better. Thanks. I guess I passed out?"

"Yes," Amos said. "We thought you'd be more comfortable on the couch in here than on the floor."

"Thanks." Carsten rubbed his head. "What do we do now?"

"You should get home before your ma worries too much," Obadiah said.

Carsten nodded. "I will, but first we need to talk. We need to bring in someone else to investigate this. We botched it tonight."

Amos shook his head. "Not completely. We know Carey Eldridge and the marshal are in on it, as well as at least one other mystery man."

Obadiah cleared his throat. "You should contact the Texas Rangers. They'll be able to take over."

Carsten hesitated. More law enforcement. What if they were corrupt, too, like the town marshal? As soon as he thought about it, he berated himself. Even if one or two were corrupt, not all of them would be. "I'll figure out how to send them a message tomorrow."

Edmund came over. "You sure? Maybe someone else should."

"No. If I need someone else, I'll have Ma come get you. Or have her send the message to the Rangers."

Kit and Amos joined Edmund. "Do you want us to walk home with you?" Edmund asked.

"No, I can get there myself."

Obadiah rested a hand on Carsten's good shoulder. "Stay safe and do not hesitate to come for help, if you need anything. Especially with the farming. Oh, and I suggest asking your ma to put together a sling for your arm and taking it easy with your shoulder for a couple of weeks."

Carsten gave a light groan. "I'll try to do that. Talk to you guys later." He stood and headed for the door. Three sets of footsteps followed him, and he turned. "Guys! I'll be fine. You can stop hovering over me."

"Sorry," Kit said. "You're hurt worse than we are. And we're concerned."

"I know. I'll take it easy for a few days."

"Weeks," Amos interrupted.

Carsten clenched his teeth. "I'll try."

"And you'll tell us when you need help?" Edmund asked.

"Of course. Don't I always?"

"No," Carsten's friends said in unison.

Carsten shook his head. "You're right. I'll do better this time. I need to get home before Ma gets too worried."

He let himself out of the house and slowly made his way home. He needed to think, and his shoulder still hurt if he went too fast. He sucked in a deep breath and instantly regretted it. No more deep breaths. His ribs still ached some unless he kept to normal or shallow breathing.

He needed to pray. God had gotten him through the last couple weeks, and He could get him through this, too.

"Ma?" There was a lamp lit on the table when Carsten opened the door.

Ma stirred on her rocking chair. "Carsten? That you? Are Amos, Edmund, and Kit with you?"

"No, they're at the Bar X Ranch."

She stood and came over. "What's wrong?"

"Nothing."

She just stared.

"Okay..." He inhaled slowly and told her everything that had happened.

Ma put a hand on his right arm. "Oh, darling. Take your shirt off and let me take a look. I'll make a sling so you can keep some pressure off that shoulder."

Carsten unbuttoned his shirt with his good hand and carefully shrugged the material off, wincing as he straightened his left arm.

Ma directed him closer to the lamp.

"Oh, my poor baby. You will have some good bruises on this arm. Let me put some salve on it."

"Thank you, Ma."

"That's what mothers are for."

He watched as Ma found the salve. He tried to ignore the pain as she rubbed the liniment on his arm and shoulder. It hurt at first, but then the aching started to get better. "What is that?"

"It's a liniment I bought a while ago. I've added a few things to it that I think will help."

"Such as?"

Ma chuckled. "You probably don't want to know."

"True. It's helping, so whatever's in it is good with me."

"Good. Now, I'm going to work on a sling for you, and I want you to sleep on your back tonight."

"Sleep? Who said I was going to sleep?"

Ma spun him so he had to look at her. "You will at least lie down. If you don't sleep, fine. But it would be good for you if you did."

"Yes, ma'am."

"And you are going to take my bed. I don't want you climbing that ladder. I will not take *no* for an answer. I've been climbing ladders a long time and can do it for a couple days. I'm not a cripple or invalid, and don't you dare say anything about my age. I'm not as spry as I was when I was your age, but I'm still able to climb ladders. Who do you think goes up to the hayloft to make the kittens tame?"

Carsten's eyes widened more with each word she said. "Yes, ma'am. I'll sleep on your bed. Or try to sleep. And I won't say another word about it."

Ma disappeared for a bit and came back with a triangular piece of cloth. "Put your arm across your chest so it is comfortable."

He did as she said.

She slipped the material under his arm and tied it around his neck. "Is that okay?"

"It'll take some getting used to, but it's fine."

"Good. Now go to bed. I'll bring your clothes down tomorrow."

"Oh!" He tapped a finger on his head. "We need to go somewhere to contact the Texas Rangers tomorrow."

"We can talk about that in the morning. Try to get some sleep."

"Yes, ma'am." He paused. "Ma. Do you know Mr. Jenkins?"

Ma spun around. "Why do you ask?"

"No reason. Just curiosity. He mentioned it when I was out there, and for some reason, all this reminded me. Probably because he looked like he got hurt a few times."

Ma smiled. "He did. When we first moved here, your pa and I had a rough go of it. Mr. Jenkins stopped by one day and helped Foster for a couple days. He seemed like a sweet man. I always wondered why he stayed a hermit."

Carsten shrugged with his good shoulder. "He didn't say.

But I'd like to go visit him again sometime. Maybe you could come with me."

"I'd love to. Now go get some sleep."

"Yes, Ma. I'll try."

Carsten went to her room and lay flat on his back on top of the blankets. He wasn't cold and shouldn't get chilled anyway. He took a deep breath and let it out, closing his eyes. Sleep. He knew he needed it, but with his mind racing the way it was, he didn't think he'd get any.

Not much later, stabbing light streamed onto his face, and he winced. He slowly opened his eyes. The sun shone in the window. He didn't have a window in his loft. Where was he? Oh. Right. Ma's room. The smell of coffee hit his nose next, and he rolled carefully out of bed. His shoulder ached, but otherwise, he wasn't terribly sore anywhere else. Even his ribs seemed better.

A fresh pair of pants and a shirt were on the chair next to the bed, and he smiled. Ma was a sneaky one. He dressed carefully and discovered how hard it was to pull pants on with one arm.

He shuffled out of the room into the main area. "Mornin'."

"Good morning, Carsten. How are you?"

"Not too bad, considering."

"I'm glad. I've been thinking. Let's go to West Prairie to send the telegram."

Ma handed him a cup of coffee, and he took a sip of it before responding. "I was thinking the same thing. I don't want to risk anyone in town knowing we're contacting the Rangers."

"Exactly. I'll come with you. I wouldn't mind seeing if there's anything new in the stores there."

"And you want to keep a close eye on me."

Ma winked. "Of course. I know you, Carsten. And I know you will overdo it at some point. I can't stop that, but I can try as much as possible to prevent you from overdoing it."

Carsten groaned. "Ma, you are too smart."

"I know."

"Well, all I need is a little something to eat, and then we can go."

"I happen to have some muffins made. But I'll whip up some eggs as well. You sit there and drink your coffee. Before we leave, I also want to rub some more liniment into your shoulder."

"Yes, ma'am."

An hour later, they were on their way. By the end of the day, the Rangers would have their message and hopefully be sending some people Carsten's way.

CHAPTER 17

Trust

Two days after Carsten sent the telegram, he sat outside sulking and watching the road. He kept seeing dust clouds that became nothing. When would the Rangers get here? Why hadn't he stayed in town to wait for a response? Surely there had to be a couple of Rangers that weren't too far away.

Carsten didn't know what to do with himself. He couldn't work on the alfalfa. He couldn't help with the branding. He couldn't even help Ma in the garden. Restless didn't even begin to describe it. He did make one delivery for Mr. Graves. It was hard to see Carey working at the print shop and not start accusing him. Especially when he saw the bruise on his face. Presumably, Carsten or one of his friends put it there.

Another dust cloud caught Carsten's eye. He shook his head. Probably an animal or something. He had to stop getting his hopes up for no reason.

The dust cloud came closer. It wasn't an animal; it was a person riding a horse. He squinted. Only one person, though. Would the Rangers send only one person? And how would they know where he lived besides a farm outside Angleton? They were investigators, so maybe they'd asked around.

As the dust cloud came closer, he realized it couldn't be a Ranger. The rider sat sidesaddle. What woman would be coming here? Or was she riding by on her way to someone else's home?

The rider and horse slowed as they neared the entrance to the Whitfords' front yard. Carsten could finally see the rider's face, and the breath left his chest.

Luella.

She dismounted in front of him, and he took the reins for her horse with his good hand and tied them loosely to the hitching post.

"Hi," he said.

She quirked a nervous smile. "Hi."

They stood awkwardly staring at each other for a minute.

"Sorry, I…"

"Me, too," she said. "We need to talk."

"Do you want to come inside?"

"Not really. I…" She looked down. "I'd prefer it be just you and me."

Carsten nodded. "Have a seat."

They sat on the step, and he waited for her to begin.

"I've been utterly unfair to you. I let my papa tell me things about you that I knew couldn't be true, but I believed him. It wasn't right. You tried to tell me that, but I didn't want to listen. I didn't want to believe Papa could be wrong."

"So you believe I am innocent?" Carsten let a little hope sneak in.

"Yes." She took a deep, shuddering breath. "I also think you might be right about Papa."

His breath caught in his chest. "What?"

"You said you think he's involved in something besides just a robbery."

"Why do you think I'm right?" Carsten asked.

"When I went to bed a few days ago, Papa was perfectly fine. When I woke up that morning, he had a scratch on his cheek and a bruise peeking out of his shirt collar. Then I heard you, Amos, Kit, and Edmund were hurt. I didn't know what to think."

"Did you say anything to your pa?"

"No."

"Good."

Luella picked at her skirt. "What is he involved with?"

Carsten hesitated. Did she really want to know? Carsten didn't have any clear evidence. "We're still investigating."

"I know. Tell me what you think he's doing." Luella turned to look at him. "Please."

Carsten sighed. "Counterfeiting money."

Luella's eyes widened, then closed, and she bowed her head. "That makes sense, actually."

Carsten's mouth fell open. "It does?"

"Yes. Papa's made some bad business deals lately and thinks Mother and I need more money than he's made recently. It's not true. We love our luxuries, but we don't absolutely need them. We've tried telling him that, but he won't listen. Counterfeiting money is the type of risk he might take."

Carsten sighed. "This is the last thing I wanted. I'm sorry."

"Me, too." Luella slumped against the porch railing. "So here's what I know. I wasn't completely honest when I told you Papa didn't leave the house after getting home from work. He sneaks out after everyone is in bed. Not every night but often enough that I've noticed it. Then a couple days ago, he had the injuries. Minor compared to yours, of course." She brushed a finger on his bad arm. "I'm sorry if he had anything to do with this."

"Thanks. Do you happen to have ideas on who he might be in league with?"

"He's been talking to the marshal and Mr. Baumgartner more often than usual, so maybe them? Or there's something going on in the town they need to talk about. Either possibility could be accurate."

"Thank you. That is helpful."

Luella opened her mouth as if to talk but then closed it again.

"What is it?"

"I… Do you have a plan on how to catch them?"

"Obadiah suggested that we contact the Texas Rangers. So I did that two days ago."

"Good." She sighed. "I'm glad we're talking again."

Carsten smiled. "Me, too."

They sat in silence for a while.

She trusted him again. It was time he trusted her with something as well. He needed to know what she would think of him if she knew the whole truth. He cleared his throat. "I need to tell you something."

Luella's big, brown eyes held a little confusion. "What is it?"

"Four years ago, I did something stupid. Childish."

"You were a child. Fourteen."

"True. But by then, I was also the man of the house."

"So this happened after your pa went to prison?"

"Yes. About three weeks after."

"So you were still reeling from your loss."

"Yes. I was out wandering and saw a palomino horse ground tied near a small camp. The owner wasn't around, and I took the horse for a ride. I was gone for less than an hour and returned the horse to the same spot. I even brushed her down. At the time, it was exhilarating.

"A week or so later, I overheard some people talking about the owner of a palomino horse and that he was dead. Ever since, I've had the nagging feeling that I'm responsible. Horse thievery is punishable by death, and I couldn't do that to Ma, so I never told anyone."

Luella looked down and played with her skirt again but

didn't respond. Carsten began to wonder if he was wrong to confide in her. Would she turn him in?

"What if he didn't die because of you? It could have been natural causes."

"True, but the timing seems too coincidental."

"Perhaps you should talk to the Rangers when they come. They can investigate and then you can accept any punishment they think is necessary."

Carsten cocked his head. "You're right. That's a great idea. I knew I liked you for a reason."

"Why?" Luella asked, a sparkle of mischief in her eyes. "Because I'm smarter than you?"

Carsten laughed. He touched his sore shoulder. "Ouch. Don't make me laugh."

Luella's smile became a frown. "Are you all right? Do you need anything to help ease the pain I caused?"

Carsten took a couple slow, deep breaths. "No. I'm fine. Or will be in a minute. My laugh was a little too boisterous for my shoulder."

Luella sighed. "I wish I didn't know one of the people who'd done this to you."

"Me, too. Your pa's a good man. He shouldn't have gotten himself involved in this."

"No, he shouldn't have. He should've talked to us, and we could have figured out something else. Hiring fewer servants. I don't mind doing some of the cooking and cleaning. I want to know how to do both anyway."

Carsten smiled. "Most of the eligible men around here won't be able to hire cooks and maids, so you'll have to do those chores if and when you get married."

Luella laughed. "That is true. I need to pick up on learning some of those things better."

"Can I walk you back home?"

"That probably isn't a great idea. I don't know where Papa

is right now. And I don't want him to know I was talking to you."

"Okay. I'll at least walk you to the magnolia tree." He stood and held out his good arm to help her up.

"Thank you."

"My pleasure. I'm just happy to be on speaking terms again. I only wish it wasn't for the reason it is."

"Mm-hm."

After untying Luella's horse's reins, Carsten led the animal and talked about little things on the way to the magnolia tree. Once there, he helped Luella mount the horse, handed her the reins, and waved goodbye. He waited until she was a tiny speck on the horizon before turning back to home.

He knew what he needed to do. Carsten couldn't let Luella go on pretending in front of her pa. It had been two days since Carsten contacted the Rangers, but they were being too slow. He needed to move this investigation along. Not today, but soon.

CHAPTER 18

Broken

The next morning, Carsten's shoulder ached a little less, so he headed out to the field and took a look at what was going on with the alfalfa. Even after almost a week of neglect, it looked good. He needed to get rid of some of the weeds, though. There were a few too many. He grabbed the hoe with his right hand and started whacking away one-handed. It didn't work very well, but it was good enough.

An hour later, he wiped the sweat off his forehead and stood at the end of the row. With a heavy sigh, he collapsed onto the ground. At this rate, the weeds would be back in this row before he finished even half the field. How was he supposed to weed when he couldn't use two arms?

Carsten could ask his friends for help. How would he repay them? He couldn't take time out of the fields to help them. At least not much. They wouldn't ask for anything in return, but that didn't mean he wouldn't want to do it anyway.

Carsten left the hoe at the edge of the field and went on his knees and weeded by hand. It was a little faster than with the hoe but still not enough. What would happen during harvest if he left some of these weeds in with the alfalfa now?

It would be poorer quality since the cattle didn't prefer their alfalfa mixed with weeds, but it might be his only option.

With a shake of his head, he stopped those thoughts. He needed to think about something else. Such as his plan to move things along faster with the investigation. Should he let it slip that counterfeiters were in town? If he did, who would believe him? Very few in town trusted him, even now. If he said something, they could turn on him instead.

He needed to do something else. A confrontation? But of whom? Carey? The marshal? Not Mr. Comstock. Carsten needed to stay in Luella's good graces. Luella. She was too good for this life. She was too good to have a father who would end up in prison right next to Carsten's pa. How could Mr. Comstock have done this? What had he been thinking?

Carsten knew how hard it was to not have a pa around. Especially when that pa was in prison. He didn't want Luella to go through that, too. She was older now than he was at the time of his pa's conviction, so maybe that would make a difference. But it still seemed so wrong for any parent to do something illegal to provide for their family. There had to be better ways.

His pa had done what he knew. He'd grown up with criminals. Mr. Comstock? There wasn't an explanation for him besides he wasn't thinking things through. At least Carsten hoped that was all it was.

He reached the end of the row and looked back. It hadn't taken quite as long but was even harder on his shoulder and knees. He stood and looked around. The weeds weren't too bad yet. Maybe in a week or two, his shoulder could take the beating from the hoe again, and he could get back to it. Or perhaps he could find another solution by then.

He wandered around the field, bending down to pick some of the worst weeds here and there. He made it to the far end of the field and stopped. There was very little he could do here. He felt helpless.

"God, I want to trust that You have everything in control, but what am I supposed to do now? I can't take care of my own fields and can't hire anyone to help me either. I need my shoulder miraculously healed, or I need help I can't pay for and the ability to not be too prideful about asking for that help. I don't know what to do anymore. I want the Rangers to fix everything, but they aren't here yet, and I'm not sure I can wait. Help me be patient and help me trust You and whoever else I need to."

Carsten made his way back to the house. As the small cabin came into view, he saw three figures coming toward him. A smile flitted onto his face, and he picked up his pace.

"You have no idea how much I needed to see you three today," Carsten said as he got closer.

Edmund pointed at Carsten's knees. "I think we might have a rough idea. What were you doin'?"

"Trying to weed my alfalfa. The hoe is too unwieldy one-handed."

Amos guffawed. "Well, we're here to help. And we even brought a couple of hoes, knowing you might need something."

"I can't—"

"Excuse me," Kit interrupted. "We are here to offer our services to a friend, and you would deny us?"

Carsten ducked his head. He appreciated their help, but he hadn't wanted it. He knew they had wounded his pride and knew that was wrong. But knowing and not being affected by it were two different things. He took a deep breath and looked up. "No. Of course not. But I'm the one who got you and myself into this position." The looks on his friends' faces made him stop talking. "Which has no relevance here. Um. Let's go."

Carsten brought them to the row he had stopped at. "I already did the first two rows. Basically anything that isn't knee-high is probably a weed."

"Perfect," Amos said. "Your job, while we work, is to keep us entertained."

Carsten blinked. "How?"

"We don't care," Edmund answered. "Talk to us? Do a song and a dance?"

Carsten laughed. "Ouch. Don't make me laugh. I won't be doing a song and dance, but I can talk. Any particular topic?"

"Anything but the investigation," Kit suggested.

"Will do." Carsten thought for a bit as they started hoeing. He could suddenly only think about the investigation. Luella. He could talk about her willingness to help them. "So this is sort of investigation related but also not completely. Luella came here yesterday. Looks like her pa is one of the counterfeiters. She heard about our injuries and realized her pa must have been part of it. He's got an unexplained scratch on his face and a bruised upper chest."

Kit sighed. "Poor girl."

"Woman," Carsten corrected. "And yes. I was really hoping we were wrong about him."

"Did she have any ideas on his motivation?" Amos asked.

He nodded before realizing they couldn't see him well. Carsten updated them on what he'd learned from Luella.

"Does this mean you and Luella are talking again?" Edmund asked.

Carsten grinned. "Yes, we are."

"And?" Amos asked.

"And what?"

"Are you courting yet?"

Carsten groaned. "Come on. Do I really have to answer that? My innocence hasn't been proven yet. If the Rangers don't get here soon to stop this ridiculous accusation, I'll end up in jail. I can't ask her now."

All three of his friends stopped hoeing and opened their mouths.

Carsten held up a hand. "Before you protest, know that I

plan to inquire as soon as all of this is over. If she'll keep talking to me after her pa gets arrested anyway."

"She's the one who told you about his involvement," Edmund said.

"That doesn't mean she's willing to let me court her afterwards. I'll still ask when the time is right. It'll be harder since neither of us will have our pas around."

"But it's doable."

"True." He bit the inside of his mouth to keep from smiling. "What about you three? Any girls we need to tease you about yet?"

Amos and Kit shook their heads, but Edmund's cheeks reddened.

Carsten raised his eyebrow. "Edmund! What are you hiding? Who's the lucky lady that caught your eye?"

Edmund glared at Carsten. "Her name is Anna. She just moved to town."

"She was at church this week, right?" Kit asked.

Edmund grinned.

"She's pretty," Amos said.

"She's mine," Edmund said.

"Oh, of course," Amos said. "I'm not interested in her at all. You can have her. Don't worry about me."

"So no one has caught your eye, Amos?" Carsten asked.

"Not yet," Amos answered.

"Too bad," Carsten said. "Why is that? You could have any girl you wanted."

"That's the problem," Amos said. "I'm the son of a rich rancher. Everyone wants a part of that, so I don't know who's interested in me and who wants me because of the money."

Carsten sighed. "I'm sorry. I didn't think about that problem."

"That's because you've never had it."

A pain stabbed into his heart. "Yeah. I guess not. Just other problems."

Amos put a hand on his arm. "Sorry. You're right. I get to have everything I want. A little hardship like not knowing who wants me for me versus my money is nothing compared to not knowing where the next meal will come from."

Carsten smiled, but his heart still hurt. "I shouldn't have taken it so personally."

"No, you're right," Amos said. "I shouldn't have said it that way."

They went back to work without him talking for a while. They each got two rows done before Carsten talked again. "You guys are fast."

"It helps that there are three of us, and we don't have injured arms," Kit said.

"True," Carsten said. "You all don't have to finish if you don't want to. Or do any more."

"We want to," Amos answered. "You need more than this done."

"Yes, but don't you have other things to do?"

Amos shrugged. "Of course, but we got permission to help you the rest of the day."

Carsten's chest tightened. He didn't want them here all day helping him out of pity. He needed help, but not out of pity. "Does that mean you have to stay the whole day?"

Amos scowled. "Where is this attitude coming from? No, we don't have to stay all day. I thought it would be a nice thing to do."

"Yeah," Kit said. "We thought you would need some help and knew you wouldn't ask for it."

"So you decided to take pity on poor Carsten?" Carsten asked. "Is that it?"

Edmund came over. "We aren't doing this out of pity; we're doing it out of friendship. Friends help each other no matter what. We know you don't have help here with your pa gone. The branding is almost done, and my pa and Kit's pa each have a ranch hand helping to pick up the slack when we need it."

Carsten growled. "I know. It's the one thing I've never understood. Why would you, a rich kid and two ranch boys, befriend a poor farmer boy like me?"

"Because," Amos answered, "we don't see you for the money you make but for your personality. You're a nice guy. Someone a lot like us. We want you to always be welcomed, and hopefully you never feel out of place around us. Besides, now that you're running the farm, I'm sure you won't be poor much longer."

"If I get arrested, I will be."

"You'll get proven innocent," Kit said. "I know you will."

Carsten grunted but didn't say anything.

"Let's go to the river to cool off," Edmund suggested.

Amos gave Carsten a pointed look, glancing at his arm.

"I can go into the water," Carsten said. "I'd have to be careful about jostling it."

"Fine. Let's go. We've gotten a few rows done each and there isn't too much left."

Carsten's brain said he needed to move, but his feet refused to obey.

"Are you coming, Carsten?" Edmund asked.

"No," Carsten replied too quickly. "I mean, I don't really want to today. Especially when I can't splash around as much. I know I said I could go in the water, but... I don't really feel like it now."

"Hopefully soon, then," Amos said. "What do we want to do in the meantime?"

"Keep hoeing," Kit said. "May as well get a good portion of this field done while we're here."

Carsten tensed. "You don't have to."

"Yes we do," Kit said. "It's what friends do for each other."

Carsten's chest tightened, but he had nothing more he

could say to dissuade them. He sat at the edge of the field and watched them hoe their respective rows. When they got back to his end of the field, he was ready to talk again. "What do you think of going to town and seeing what our suspects are up to? Maybe seeing who else was injured."

"I thought we were waiting for the Rangers," Amos said.

"It's been almost four days since I sent the telegram," Carsten replied. "They're sure taking their sweet time about getting here."

"They're busy. Or maybe they needed to gather special supplies," Kit said.

Carsten scowled. "I'm getting too impatient not being able to do anything. Walking is about the only physical activity I can do with little pain. I need to do something!" He looked into each of his friends' faces, or rather tried to, but they were all looking down. "Well? Is there something I can do that I haven't thought of?"

"We shouldn't have trusted Carsten," Edmund muttered.

The comment cut straight through Carsten's heart, knocking him backwards a few steps. "Excuse me?"

Edmund looked up with a grimace. "I meant we shouldn't have trusted that you would let us help you here in the fields, Carsten."

"Go," Carsten said through gritted teeth, pointing to the road. "Leave my farm and don't think about coming back." His hands shook, and it was all he could do to not yell at them. They didn't trust him? He thought out of everybody, they believed in him. But now it turned out he had been wrong all along. Again. As soon as they were out of sight, Carsten tried to stand and collapsed instead. His friends were gone, and he let the tears fall unchecked.

CHAPTER 19

Confrontation

Carsten didn't say a word to Ma about what had happened with his so-called friends. He couldn't bear to admit it out loud or hear all her explanations. He went through his day in a daze, trying to get things done and failing again and again. Trying not to run through everything his friends had said.

Everything inside him told him he needed to go to town and confront the marshal. Give him a piece of his mind. God wasn't working fast enough. The Rangers weren't coming. Or if they were, they were taking too long. Carsten couldn't wait any longer. He needed to do something.

After Ma went to bed, he carefully and quietly slid down the ladder. He'd made Ma return to her room a couple days earlier. Sliding down the ladder meant he could go one-handed. Now all he needed to do was manage not to get even more injured when confronting the marshal.

The door creaked ever so slightly as he opened it, and he winced. No noise came from Ma's room, though, so he slipped through the door and closed it gently.

Carsten hurried down the road. He wanted to make sure he said what he needed to and get home before Ma knew he was gone. A thought niggled at his mind, but he shut it out. Prayer was out of the question right now.

He knew what he was doing was wrong. He wasn't trusting God to work, and he didn't want to. He needed this to be over for himself, and especially for Luella.

Carsten stopped under the magnolia tree to rest for a minute. His arm was doing better but still ached, as did his ribs. He took it out of the sling and did a slow rotation. A grunt escaped before he could hold it back. It hurt but wasn't as bad as he'd thought it would be. Maybe he could get back to work sooner than he thought.

Shaking the stray thoughts away, he continued his trek to town. He wanted to get there before the marshal started his midnight rounds. If he did them at all. If the marshal could be a counterfeiter, maybe he slacked off on his duties around town as well. Maybe he could be arrested and fired for negligence.

Carsten's brain went to odd places when left unchecked.

He approached the marshal's office, walking in the shadows so no one would see him. It took longer, but speed wasn't everything here. When he reached the marshal's door, he paused and listened for a minute. He didn't hear anyone talking, so if the marshal was inside, he was likely alone. Carsten took a deep breath and opened the door.

He stepped inside and glanced around. No one. He let out a sigh. Now all he had to do was wait for the marshal to come back. Carsten sat on the chair by the door and prepared himself to be stuck alone for a while.

The solid door to the cells rattled, and he jumped. Had someone been in there all along? Carsten hopped up and winced at the pain in his shoulder. The door opened, and Carsten wiped the wince off his face.

Marshal Lydick stepped in from the back, and it pleased Carsten to see him startled.

"Evenin', Marshal," he said.

"You can almost say *mornin'*," the marshal stated.

"True."

The marshal went behind his desk and sat. "What can I do for you?"

Carsten stepped closer and kept standing. "I came to ask you a few questions."

Marshal Lydick narrowed his eyes. "About what?"

"Why did you accuse me of a robbery I didn't commit?"

"There is no proof you didn't."

"No, but there also isn't proof I did. You never found the missing paper in my house, and if I had stolen paper, I would have hidden it in the house. Anywhere else would have been a terrible idea. Instead, what my friends and I have found out is much worse. And I think you're a part of it."

"Found out? What do you think you have found out?"

Carsten swallowed. Did he dare say it? Or did he wait for the Rangers to arrive? "I'm not ready to say more than that right now. Just know we've found out a few things that are rather incriminating. And I still want an answer as to why you would accuse me of stealing that paper. I would have no use for fancy paper, and if I did, I would have paid for it. When I stole things, it was little trinkets, not paper. And certainly not from a store."

The marshal sat staring at him but said nothing.

"You don't even have an excuse? Nothing that would justify accusing an innocent man?" Carsten lifted his arm as best he could with the sling. "Hurting him because he almost caught you and your conspirators? That's really the best you can do?"

Marshal Lydick still said nothing but did scowl.

"You're supposed to be a trustworthy person. Someone everyone can count on. Not the villain. The person who goes around scheming about how he can get away with his own misdeeds. The marshal's job is to protect the citizens of the town, not hurt or falsely accuse them."

The scowl on the marshal's face deepened, and his hands clenched into fists.

"You are really going to sit there and not say a word?"

Nothing.

Carsten gritted his teeth. "I guess I'll leave for now and come back another time for answers. Or wait..." He stopped himself. The marshal couldn't find out about the Rangers. That would be too dangerous. He could cover up most of the evidence. He needed to think it was Carsten and his three friends he had to worry about, not anyone else. "Or wait until I can get my friends to join me." Carsten's stomach clenched. Could he even count on his friends' help or want it? "Maybe if the four of us confront you, you'll actually..."

Before Carsten could finish the sentence, the marshal knocked his chair over and came around the desk. Carsten barely saw the fist coming at him in time to raise his good arm to block it. He was smaller and nimbler, and all his agility did was save him some pain. Carsten somehow managed to get his arm out of the sling, but between the blows hitting him and his shoulder, the pain became too much. Blackness threatened to engulf him, but he fought it off as long as he could.

Blows hit his head, his body, everywhere. He blocked them and tried to get a few blows in himself but couldn't. The door to the cells was open, and he managed to get in there, somewhere hearing a man shouting something about the marshal beating up a defenseless boy. Had someone else come in to help him? No. The alcohol infiltrated his nostrils. It was a drunk in a cell.

Mercifully, the blows stopped as Carsten stumbled in and fell in front of one of the cells.

Blackness kept descending. He was helpless to stop it. A hand touched his good shoulder as he lay on his back on the floor.

"You all right, kid?" an echoey voice asked.

Carsten couldn't answer. It was all he could do to breathe and fight off the darkness. As his vision narrowed, he saw a new figure step into the office. Was that Mr. Comstock?

The man glanced toward Carsten and back to the marshal.

Darkness filled Carsten's vision, but his hearing worked by fits and starts another minute.

"… safe."

"… not safe… looking… friends."

"… plates…"

THE FIRST THING Carsten noticed was his cold and numb fingers. Then the stiffness in his body and light through his eyelids. Carsten groaned and tried to stretch. His arms wouldn't move. Panicked, he tried to open his eyes only for them to refuse to open. What was wrong with him? He concentrated hard and managed to open his eyes. It was still dark out, but there was just enough light from the lanterns in the office so that he could start seeing a few things. Outlines. Shapes. He could hear snoring. Was he still in a jail cell?

Carsten tried to move his arms again, but they were still stuck behind him. Then he felt something on his wrists, and he glanced back as much as he could. The end of a rope was visible behind him. Someone had tied him up.

"Hey. You're awake," a voice near him said.

Carsten glanced over at the previously snoring man. "Barely," Carsten rasped. He cleared his throat. "What happened?"

"Marshal beat you up pretty good, then Mr. Comstock came in and tied you up. Why're they doin' this to you?"

"I know something about them they don't want anyone else to hear."

"Hm. Well. Good to see you're alive. Can you get out of here?"

Carsten strained to move his arms. "I don't think so. I can barely move and certainly can't slip out of the ropes. They're tied too well." He groaned. How could he have been so reckless? Confronting the marshal about his part in the counterfeiting while Carsten himself had an injury?

Darkness threatened again, and he sucked in a long breath. "Talk to me. I can't go unconscious again. Why are you here?"

The man chuckled. "I got drunk last night, and the marshal put me in here for my own safety."

"And because you wouldn't leave the saloon on your own?" Carsten asked.

"I don't actually remember for sure. I only know I ended up here and saw your fight last night."

"Would you be willing to tell..." Carsten glanced at the now-shut door. "Would you be willing to tell someone else what happened last night?"

The drunk nodded. "But who?"

Carsten rolled onto his right side and whispered, "Texas Rangers are coming any day now."

"I've never seen any o' them before."

"Me neither. But hopefully they'll be here soon."

"You look like you'll need any help you can get."

Carsten's head pounded, and his vision darkened again. He groaned as a new wave of pain rolled over him.

"You all right?" His companion's voice sounded far away.

Carsten tried to respond but couldn't.

"Help!" the drunk called. "Is anyone out there to help us?"

Carsten tried to fight off the pain and stay conscious, but he lost the battle again, and the rattle of bars and shouts of a drunk were the last thing he remembered.

CHAPTER 20
Saved

Half a day's ride from Angleton, Texas

The telegram had come days ago. Lonzo Hossman tapped his foot impatiently. He was the farthest from being in charge, but also the only one of the three Rangers assigned to the case who seemed to think the young man who'd sent the telegram might be in more danger than it appeared.

Casper and Zachariah wanted to wait until dawn to finish the short ride to town, but Lonzo had a sense that something had happened that needed their attention right away. He'd tried to say so the night before, but Casper and Zachariah were older and wanted their rest. Lonzo knew how reckless young men his age could be. He feared Carsten and his friends might do something and get into trouble.

Lonzo rose from his spot on the ground and stirred up the campfire. At least he could make sure the coffee was hot and have a small breakfast prepared so they could leave as soon as they finished.

By the time dawn broke the horizon, Lonzo had the coffee

and food ready and dished up. "Time to wake up if you don't want your food getting cold."

Zachariah groaned. "You're really that concerned?"

"Yes."

"Fine. Casper!" Zachariah poked at the man next to him. "Get up. We'll eat, pack up camp, and head to town."

"I just went to sleep," Casper complained.

"Hours ago," Lonzo stated. "Eat your food, or I'll eat it for you."

"You wouldn't dare," Casper said.

Lonzo raised an eyebrow. "Wouldn't I?"

Casper sat up and flung his blanket away, grabbing for his coffee and remaining beans.

Lonzo chuckled softly. He wouldn't have actually eaten Casper's food but knew how much the man liked to eat. It was a good motivator.

Thankfully Casper and Zachariah ate quickly. Lonzo finished before them and started packing up the camp. The sun bathed them in light as they doused the fire with the remaining coffee and mounted up.

The ride to the town was a quiet one. Lonzo would have gladly talked about their plan but waited for Zachariah to bring it up. But when buildings came into view, Lonzo reined his horse in. "What is our plan?"

"We'll go to the marshal's office," Zachariah said.

"But I thought Carsten said the marshal was one of them."

"Yes, but it is common courtesy anyway. We won't tip our hand and let him know we know. We will simply tell him we are in town investigating a small matter and then try to find this Carsten boy."

Lonzo's stomach fluttered. He hoped Zachariah was right. They continued into town, and Lonzo spotted the marshal's office in the middle of town. The sign was obvious and a little pretentious. Had the town or the marshal himself put it there?

They stopped in front of the marshal's office and

dismounted in unison. Lonzo followed Zachariah and Casper to the door.

Before Zachariah opened the door, Lonzo tapped his shoulder. "Wait. Listen."

"Help!" a voice came from inside the office. "Someone help us."

Zachariah opened the door and burst into the marshal's office.

Lonzo followed quickly. No marshal. He saw the door to his right and opened it slowly. A prone and bound form caught Lonzo's attention immediately. "Casper, go get the doctor. Now!"

"You the Rangers Carsten said were coming?" a man to Lonzo's right asked.

"Yes," Lonzo answered. "Who are you?"

"No one important, but my name is Cooper Burda. Just a drunk who saw the marshal beat up poor Carsten. Kid's been through a lot, what with his pa teachin' him to steal, then gettin' sent to jail. The boy was fourteen when he became the man of the house and had to keep the farm goin'."

"Wait. This is Carsten?"

"Yes it is."

Lonzo cut the ropes and laid Carsten on his back. "Why is he unconscious?"

"He didn't say. I'd guess from the pain."

Zachariah came in with keys rattling. "I assume you can get out now that it's morning and you've sobered up?"

Cooper chuckled. "Yes, sir. I was waitin' for the marshal to come by but haven't seen hide nor hair since he left Carsten here."

Zachariah moved past Lonzo and unlocked the cell. "You saw the marshal beat Carsten up?"

"Yes."

"And you're willing to give a statement?"

"Yes."

A commotion sounded in the other room, and Lonzo turned to see the doctor coming in. Zachariah and Cooper stepped out of the hallway and let the doctor in.

"What happened here?" the doctor asked.

"He got beat up," Lonzo stated.

"Who is…" The doctor stopped. "Carsten? What is he doing here? Where is the marshal?"

"Just fix him up, Doc; we'll investigate the other questions. Cooper Burda said he was conscious for a little while but then went limp."

"Help me get him on his back," the doctor said.

Lonzo did as he said and stood to get out of the way.

"Stay down here," the doctor said. "I might need your help."

Lonzo crouched down and watched the doctor check everywhere on Carsten's body.

"Shoulder's still injured but not worse," the doctor muttered. "No broken ribs, don't think there's internal bleeding, no broken limbs. The head injury is the only thing to worry about. I need that rag wet."

Lonzo grabbed the rag, jumped up, and went to the other room. A quick glance around showed a bucket of water near the door. He dunked the rag in and squeezed it to get the excess water out, then brought it back to the doctor.

The doctor worked on Carsten.

After a while, Carsten stirred with a groan.

"Carsten, can you hear me?" the doctor asked.

Carsten groaned. "Doc?" His eyes fluttered open. "Where am I?"

"The marshal's office. Do you remember what happened?"

Carsten slowly sat up. "Yes." He looked around and locked eyes with Lonzo. "Who are you?"

"Texas Ranger Lonzo Hossman."

"You finally arrived? Thank God!"

"When you're ready, we'll have questions for you."

Carsten nodded. "I need to go home and check on Ma first. Let her know I'm all right."

"The furthest you will go is my office or a hotel," the doctor said. "I want you to be close so I can stop in throughout the day. Do you think Luella would be willing to get your ma for you?"

"Yes," Carsten said.

"I'll ask her to go to the farm to talk to your ma."

Carsten sighed. "Thank you. I guess I'll be available to answer questions all day then, Ranger Hossman. What do you need to know?"

"Please call me Lonzo."

Carsten nodded. "Yes, sir."

"Shall we go sit down to talk?" Lonzo asked.

"Sitting in a chair might be nice."

"Or maybe lying down on a bed?" the doctor asked.

"Maybe, but please, not here."

Lonzo tapped his foot on the floor. "Let me talk to Zachariah. I have an idea."

THE RANGERS WERE HERE. Carsten was alive and stuck in town for the day. But that gave him plenty of time to tell the Rangers everything he knew.

Carsten heard Lonzo talking to someone in the marshal's office. Then the voices went silent and three men came in, including the young Ranger.

"Is there a hotel in town?" the largest man asked.

"Yes," Carsten answered.

"We will get two rooms, and you can stay in one with Lonzo protecting you," the large man said. "I'm Zachariah. I will be taking charge of the investigation. Casper"—he looked at the stocky man—"you go with the man from the jail cell.

He can show you where the hotel is, and you can get us two rooms. Doc, can Carsten walk on his own?"

"He should be able to," the doctor said. "I would keep someone close in case his head injury is worse than I thought."

"Lonzo"—Zachariah took charge again—"you stay by Carsten's side all day. You can get all the information we need from him. I'll track down the marshal. Our friend from the cell said he was with a Mr. Comstock?"

Carsten's heart sank. "Yes. Doctor, when you go to Luella's, can you bring Zachariah so he can question Mr. Comstock?"

"This Luella," Zachariah questioned, "who is she?"

"Mr. Comstock's daughter, sir," Dr. Close answered.

"And friends with you, Carsten?"

Carsten tried to nod, but his head throbbed as he did so, and he inhaled. "She may be able to tell you some things as well, though I'll be sharing what she already told me."

"Everyone knows what to do, so go to it!" Zachariah said.

Casper and Carsten's cell friend left first. Lonzo and Dr. Close helped Carsten stand up. Carsten stayed in one place while he waited for the room to stop spinning.

"Could I have some water, please?" Carsten asked.

Dr. Close kept a hand on his arm, and Lonzo went to the water bucket. When he returned, he lifted the ladle to Carsten's lips.

Carsten sipped slowly, easing his dry throat. "Thank you."

"Ready to go to the hotel?" Lonzo asked.

"Yes."

"I'll be by every couple hours to check on you. If he needs anything"—Dr. Close turned to Lonzo—"come find me."

"Yes, sir."

Carsten was assisted out of the marshal's office. "Thank you for coming to help."

"That's what we're here for." Lonzo glanced at Carsten. "I

hope this doesn't come across wrong, but why were you in the marshal's office so late at night?"

Carsten grunted. "Being stupid. I confronted the marshal, but I shouldn't have. I'm grateful you all showed up when you did."

Lonzo was quiet as if deep in thought. "Any idea where the marshal would have gone?"

"Not really. I think I know who is involved but don't know for sure about two of them. One is bigger than the average man, so probably Theodore Baumgartner. The other…" Carsten sighed. "The other, I think, is the father of a friend of mine. Luella Comstock." He stopped. "I did hear something about the word *safe*. Could mean they felt safe or have something to do with the safe. I don't know."

"We'll check the safe in the marshal's office, in case there is something."

They reached the hotel, and Casper met them inside with a key to the room. Once in the room, Carsten lay down on the bed and closed his eyes for a minute.

"You need a rest?" Lonzo asked.

"No, let's talk. I'll tell you everything I know." It took Carsten a while to tell him everything from the false arrest to Kit's finding the fake money to Carsten's attempt to confront the marshal.

Lonzo looked down at the notes he'd taken. "This is great. We've investigated cases with a lot less before."

A thought popped into Carsten's head, and he almost blurted it out, but instead, he held it in for a while first. "Anything else?"

"No, you rest. I'll check in with Zachariah and see if he needs any help. You should be safe here without me."

"Weren't you supposed to stay with me?"

"Yes, but I'm sure he won't mind with you being behind a locked door."

"Are you sure no one will come for me here?" Carsten asked.

"I can't guarantee anything."

Carsten's stomach knotted up. "I know." He hesitated. "Can I ask you to look into something else unrelated?"

Lonzo cocked his head. "Sure."

"I..." Carsten paused. "Four years ago, I saw a horse ground tied by a small camp. A palomino. A breed of horse I'd always wanted. I took a short ride and returned the horse back to the spot, even brushed it down so the owner wouldn't know I took her. A while later, I heard that the owner of a palomino had died. I've always wondered, and been afraid, that I was the cause."

"There're lots of reasons for someone to die. It might not have been you. I'll look into it."

"Thank you."

Lonzo put a hand on his shoulder. "Rest if you can."

"Thanks."

He left, and Carsten relaxed. His part was over. He could rest easy. No more worrying about who might come after him next. He closed his eyes and drifted off into a restful sleep.

CHAPTER 21
Investigation

Knock, knock. A persistent knocking woke Carsten up. He groaned and rolled out of bed, cradling his left arm. "Who's there?"

"Doc Close."

He stepped down with a groan. "Say a few more words, please, doctor."

"You need to be careful; I understand that. Have you been able to rest?"

He was the doctor. Not an imposter. Carsten opened the door and let him in.

"Looks like I woke you up."

"You did," Carsten answered. "I'm a bit better, though. Did Luella go out to see my ma?"

"See for yourself."

Ma stepped into the room and folded him into a hug. "I was so worried when you didn't come home. I don't want to know what you did. I'm happy you are all right."

"Me, too, Ma."

Dr. Close poked and prodded Carsten. "How's the head feel?"

"It hasn't hurt since I woke up."

"Good. Give it a bit more time. It might not stay feeling fine, but I think you'll be all right. I'll check on you again after lunch, and then you'll be free to go home when the Rangers say you are."

"Thank you, Doc," Carsten said.

Dr. Close left.

"What were you thinking?" Ma asked.

"I wasn't," Carsten said. "I... I was upset."

"Why? You don't usually get this upset over anything."

"I know. It wasn't smart. I won't do it again. I was impatient and then Edmund said something that got me a little angry, and it all boiled up into this. But I'm fine now, and I want to put it all behind me."

Ma nodded. "Do you need anything to eat?"

Before Carsten could open his mouth, his stomach growled.

Ma laughed. "I'll take that as a *yes* and go get you something."

"Don't spend too much. Something simple is fine."

"I'll spoil my son if I want to. Within reason, of course. I know we're low on money." Ma left.

Carsten sat down on the bed, then leaned his back on the headboard. Now if only Lonzo would come back with word that they caught everyone in the counterfeiting ring. And also if he could tell Carsten about the man he had borrowed the palomino from, his day would be complete. But it was still early. Carsten hoped the marshal hadn't gone to all of his conspirators and convinced them to flee.

What would Mr. Graves do? He would have to hire someone else when they arrested Carey. Why was Carsten worrying about Mr. Graves? Of everybody, he should worry more about Luella. What would her ma and she do? He would help if he could. The church would help, too. He hoped.

Even if Carsten's innocence was declared, he wanted to

find out about the horse's owner. What if Carsten had caused the palomino's owner to die? Would he go to jail or worse?

A gentle knock came through the door.

"Come in."

Ma entered with a plate of food. "The hotel owner told me the Rangers were paying for everything to do with your stay, including the food."

"That is kind of them but unnecessary."

Ma shrugged. "I agree, but if you have an issue with it, you can talk to your Ranger friends. After you eat."

"Yes, ma'am." Carsten took the plate and dug into the food after a quick prayer. Chicken wasn't his favorite, but today it was perfect. He was too hungry to worry about personal preference.

"Will you be able to harvest the alfalfa?"

Carsten's heart sank. His shoulder throbbed more than it had when he left home last night. "I don't know. I doubt it. It's too physical of a job for this bum shoulder of mine."

Ma sighed. "No matter what happens, we'll figure out something. Maybe you can barter with someone. You do one-armed work for someone, and they harvest the alfalfa when it's ready."

"What about the weeding?"

"Your friends were out helping a few days ago. Perhaps they could come again."

Carsten shook his head. "We're not on good speaking terms at the moment."

Ma looked at him, concern in her eyes. "Why?"

He told her about the argument. "I know I was wrong. I don't think he really meant it. But it stung, and I was rather harsh in my response."

"You have been under a lot of stress. I think they will forgive you. Especially if you go and tell them you forgive them."

Carsten put his feet over the edge of the bed and leaned to give Ma a hug. "You are a wise woman, Ma. Thank you."

IT WAS NEARING dinnertime when Lonzo returned to the hotel room. "We caught everybody. There were four—the town marshal, Mr. Baumgartner, Mr. Comstock, and Mr. Eldridge. Mr. Comstock gladly gave up everyone and their likely hiding places."

"How did you manage that?" Carsten asked. Ma sat next to him on the bed and patted his hand.

Lonzo smiled. "Zachariah offered him a lighter sentence. We think any judge will gladly take our recommendation since he was forthcoming on their operation."

"He wanted to be out sooner," Carsten said, "so he can still see his wife and daughter."

"Yes. We have also found most of the counterfeit money except whatever has already circulated in town. Carey admitted that he stole the paper at the marshal's insistence so they could frame you. They thought people were going to figure out what they were doing and had to find someone else to blame."

"Instead, they got me and my friends curious enough to figure it out when we wouldn't have otherwise."

"Exactly," Lonzo said. "I'm still looking into that other matter but have one other place to check. I'm headed over there now, and then you will be free to go home."

"Thank you."

Lonzo left again.

Ma turned to Carsten. "What matter?"

"I'll tell you later," Carsten said. "That was all excellent news."

"Mm-hm. I'm going home to make a celebratory supper for you."

"Thank you, Ma. I love you."

"I love you, too, dear. Be careful with that arm of yours."

"Yes, ma'am."

She left, and Carsten stood. Now that he knew no one would ambush him anywhere in town, he wanted to stretch his legs.

Carsten left the hotel room, then went down the stairs and out into the bright sunlight. Before he knew it, he had unconsciously walked to Luella's home. Carsten slumped. He was the last person she would want to see. Why had he come this way? One more bad decision in less than a day. He turned and took two steps before hearing his name.

"Carsten, wait!"

He spun to see Luella heading toward him. "Luella. I didn't mean to come here…"

"Why not?" Luella stopped in front of him. "I knew before the Rangers came that Papa would get arrested. It had nothing to do with you."

"It had everything to do with me." Carsten ducked his head.

Luella used one finger to lift his chin. "Papa made his own choices. And we now have something else in common. If anything, I need to apologize to you. Come, let's sit on the porch swing."

Carsten placed Luella's arm around his good one and walked with her to the swing. "Why do you need to apologize?"

"For believing all the lies going around town about you. I know you better than that. I never should have thought you could do something like that. Steal paper? That isn't what you did back when you were stealing things. I had my doubts, but I buried them because I wanted my papa to be right. I am so ashamed."

"Don't be. I was ashamed after my pa's arrest too. It took me a while to realize that just because your parents make mistakes doesn't mean you will make those same mistakes. You need to learn from your parents and trust that, with God's help, you can make better choices."

Luella smiled. "You really think so?"

"I know so. If the last few weeks have taught me anything, it's exactly that."

"Thank you, Carsten. You're a very wise man."

Carsten laughed. "Not all the time. Last night, I was very unwise."

"Nobody's perfect," Luella teased.

"Especially me."

They sat in silence for a while before he sighed. "I should go back to the hotel. Lonzo was looking into the palomino owner's death and should have answers soon."

"Let me know what he finds out."

"Would you want to come with me?"

Luella hesitated. "Let me ask Mother first."

"Of course. How is she doing?"

"She took it hard, but Papa was able to talk to her, and she's doing better now."

"Good. I'll wait until you come out."

"Thanks." She darted into the house.

He stood so they could leave when she got back.

Two minutes later, Luella came out, a shawl around her shoulders. "Mother said yes, as long as I wore a shawl in case it got chilly."

"Sounds like your ma. Always worried about you."

"Yours too."

"True."

They walked in the direction of the hotel.

"Tomorrow is going to be a hard day," Luella said.

"Why?"

"We have to tell our cook and maid we can't afford to have them work for us. They rely on us to support their families. I don't know what they'll do."

"Mr. Graves will be looking to hire someone to replace Carey. Maybe one of them could take his place."

Luella smiled up at him. "I'll suggest it. Do you think he'd hire a woman?"

Carsten shrugged. "I don't know. He hired a former thief accused of stealing paper. He also was one of the few who believed I could be innocent."

"Do you think he knew somehow that Carey was involved?"

"I think Mr. Graves is a very trusting man who doesn't get suspicious about things. It was only after we discovered the counterfeit money that I suspected Carey."

They reached the hotel and found Lonzo waiting outside.

"There you are," he said. "Miss Comstock, a pleasure to see you again. Carsten, can we talk?"

"Sure. You can say anything about it in front of Luella. She knows and is the one who encouraged me to talk to a Ranger about it."

Lonzo looked around. The townspeople were all preparing for dinner, so the streets were fairly empty. "The owner of the horse died of natural causes here in town. I talked to Dr. Close, and he remembered the man. He said one of the maids at the hotel found the man in his room. He died in his sleep after living a long and full life. In fact, his horse is still in Dr. Close's care."

"Dr. Close's care? Why?" Luella asked.

Lonzo handed Carsten a piece of paper.

"What's this?" Carsten asked.

"A note from the man to the 'boy who took excellent care of my horse.'"

Carsten looked from the note to Lonzo. "He saw me?"

"Yes. He explains everything in the note. I think he knew he was about to die."

Carsten shook Lonzo's hand. "Thank you for everything. You have no idea how guilty I have felt the last four years."

Lonzo grinned. "I have an idea, but that is a long time to not know what's going on. Can I come out to your farm someday?"

"Sure. Are you sticking around?"

"Someone needs to be the law and order 'round here, and Zachariah told the mayor he'd be happy to let me stay until they find someone else."

"I'm glad," Carsten said. "You'll do a great job."

"Thanks," Lonzo said as he headed to the marshal's office.

Luella tugged on Carsten's sleeve. "What does the note say?"

Carsten chuckled. "Impatient, are you?"

Luella smirked. "Aren't you curious?"

"Of course." He unfolded the paper and started to read. "'To the boy who took excellent care of my horse, I saw you mount up and start a ride and thought maybe you were a horse thief. But the way you approached my beloved Stardust made me question myself. So I waited. You weren't gone long. Out of curiosity, I waited until after you tied her up. To my surprise, you brushed her down and left her in better shape than you found her. If you get this and I've passed on, I'd want you to become the owner of my sweet Stardust.

"'Jesse Sween.'" Carsten looked up, astonishment filling his chest. "Did I read that right?"

Luella took the paper from him and skimmed it. "You did. You own the horse you coveted. Oh, Carsten, you deserve this and so much more."

Carsten took a deep breath. "I think I'll come back into town tomorrow to talk to Dr. Close about it."

"Did I hear my name?" a jovial voice asked.

Carsten turned as the doctor stepped up next to him. "You did."

"Is this about the fair horse in my stable?"

Carsten nodded.

"Excellent. I know you may need to take a few days before

you can care for Stardust, so when you're ready, come by and get her."

"Thanks, Doc. I need to get home to Ma."

"I know. But first, I want to check that you're still all right."

Carsten consented to another poking and prodding.

After a minute, the doctor declared him fit as a fiddle.

"Thanks, Doc. Can I go home now?"

"Yes, sir."

"I'll see you soon, Luella."

Luella waved. "Bye, Carsten."

CHAPTER 22

Friendship

C arsten burst into the house to blurt out his news to Ma but instead found her with his three friends. "Um. Hi, everybody."

"I want to apologize," Edmund said. "What I said was wrong, and I never should have—"

"I know," Carsten interrupted. "My reaction was wrong, too. It had been a difficult day not being able to work, and I wasn't willing to listen to you."

"Can you forgive me?" Edmund asked.

"I already have," Carsten said. He gave Edmund a light punch to the shoulder. "Is that why all of you are here?"

"That, and because your Ma told us everyone's arrested," Amos said.

Ma shrugged with a sheepish smile. "I figured they would want to know, and I knew you needed to forgive them right away."

"Thanks, Ma," Carsten said, crossing the room to give her a hug. "Can we eat? I've actually got something to tell you all while we eat."

"There's more?" Kit asked.

"Yes, but I need food first," Carsten said.

Carsten and his friends helped Ma get the food on the table and then sat down. Carsten gave a hearty thanks for the day and the food. They all took a few bites, and then Carsten couldn't wait any longer to share what was going on. He first told them about how he had found and ridden Stardust and the guilt he'd lived with since.

"Carsten," Ma said. "Why did you never tell me?"

"I was too guilty. I didn't dare tell you, or I would have had to turn myself in. I couldn't do that. Not with Pa gone."

Kit nudged Carsten. "So what happened? Why are you suddenly so… happy?"

Carsten grinned. "Well, I asked Lonzo, one of the Rangers, to look into it for me." He paused to take another bite.

"And?" Amos asked.

"The man died in his sleep and gave me his horse."

Jaws dropped to the floor all around the table, and Carsten chuckled.

"He gave you his horse? By name?" Kit asked.

"No, by identification. As 'the boy who took excellent care of my horse.' All I need to do is get Stardust from the doctor's stable, and I'll be the proud owner of a beautiful palomino horse."

Ma rested a hand on his arm. "God is taking good care of you, son."

Carsten's eyes were wet, and he blinked a few times to keep the tears away. "Yes, He is."

Later that night, after they helped Ma clean up supper and after his friends left, Carsten sat down with Ma. She did some sewing, while he stared into the fire.

"The last few years without Pa have been hard."

"Yes, they have," Ma stated. "But you have been a young man of integrity the whole time, and I'm proud of you for that."

"Thanks, Ma. It's been hard believing I could be the one to break the chain of criminal behavior."

"Your pa never did believe me when I told him either. He always said it was a birthright. Something his grandfather and father instilled in all their children." She sighed. "I always wonder if that's why you're the only child who survived infancy."

"God helped us break it. Even when I didn't put my trust in Him all the time, He still kept me safe in His arms."

"He's good at that," Ma said with a smile.

CARSTEN COULDN'T WAIT to get Stardust. The next morning, he woke up, ate a quick breakfast, and practically ran to town.

"Carsten!" Dr. Close exclaimed as Carsten approached the doctor's office. "You're here early."

"I came to pick up Stardust."

Dr. Close chuckled. "Anxious to see her after so long?"

"Yes, sir. Thank you for keeping her."

"Happy to. She's a good horse and easy to care for."

"Do you want anything to pay for her care?"

Dr. Close shook his head. "Certainly not. Every little bit I spent was worth it. She came with the saddle that's in the barn and the halter she's wearing. You are welcome to both. I need to go check on Mrs. Bailey. She's getting close with baby number six."

Carsten smiled. "Thank you again, Doc." He waited for the doctor to leave before he headed out behind the office to the barn and went inside the corral. Stardust stood there as if waiting for him. He rubbed her nose and took hold of her halter.

"You're mine now, Stardust," Carsten whispered. "I get to take you home with me." He led her out of the corral to the barn, where the doctor put the saddle on, tightened it, and helped him mount up. He rode out of Dr. Close's yard and down the street.

Lonzo was outside the marshal's office and waved.

Carsten waved back, holding the reins loosely in his left arm, which was still in the sling, so it made riding a horse a little tricky. No one tried to stop him, and when he got past the last houses in town, he kneed Stardust into a trot. The trot didn't last long. It jarred his shoulder too much. Even at a walk, his trip home was twice as fast as normal. Horses could definitely go faster than humans. It would save a lot of time to have a horse he could consistently ride. Their workhorse was getting old, and Carsten needed her for helping in the fields, so he rarely rode her.

Ma was in the garden when he arrived. She looked up and stared. "Is that Stardust?"

He dismounted and led Stardust closer. "Yes."

Ma came over and patted Stardust's shoulder. "She's beautiful."

He sighed. "I would spend all day with her, but I need to get some other work done."

Ma smiled. "Go to it. I'll be in the garden, if you need anything."

"Thanks, Ma." Carsten led Stardust to the corral, took the saddle off, and brushed her down. Then he went out to the fields to check on the alfalfa. Amos, Edmund, and Kit were already out there, arguing and hoeing the weeds away for him. Carsten smiled. They were the best friends a man could have.

AFTER AN UNEVENTFUL WEEK, Carsten was ready for something new. He also wanted to spend more time with Luella. Now that he knew he wouldn't be arrested for anything, he wanted to move their relationship forward.

"Ma, I'm going to town to talk to Luella for a while."

"Okay, be back for lunch, please. Bring her with you if she's available."

Carsten grinned. "Yes, ma'am!"

He headed out the door. When he got to the road, he stopped. Someone was coming toward him riding sidesaddle. Very few women in this town actually rode sidesaddle, saying it was too uncomfortable.

This rider had to be Luella.

He waited for her to come closer, then greeted her with a smile.

"Where are you going, Carsten?" Luella asked.

"To come see you. We must have had the same idea, but you had it sooner than me."

Luella giggled. "It's been a week since Papa's arrest, and I needed someone to talk to."

"Would you want to take a ride around the farm?"

"Yes, please."

"I should tell Ma about my change of plans."

Luella dismounted. "I'll tell her while you saddle your horse."

"Thank you."

"I want to talk to her anyway, so I have ulterior motives."

Carsten chuckled. "See you out by the barn soon." He took the reins from Luella and led her horse back to the house and around to the barn. By the time Luella joined him, he had saddled Stardust.

They rode around the edge of the alfalfa field.

"I know it's mostly green, but alfalfa always seems prettier than other crops," Luella said.

"I've always thought so, too, but assumed it was my prejudice."

"How does it feel to not have a jail sentence awaiting you?"

Carsten looked at her. "Freeing. I can think about the future again."

"You hadn't before?"

Carsten shrugged. "I had, but I only turned eighteen a few months ago so hadn't really put anything into action yet. I wanted to be stabler first."

"What kinds of things did you want to take action on? If you don't mind my asking."

They approached the back of the alfalfa field. "I don't mind. See that thin line of blue out there?"

Luella nodded.

"That's the edge of the property. Pa never did anything with this back five acres. I want to expand and maybe even start a new type of crop."

"Any ideas on the crop?"

"Not yet. I'm thinking wheat if my arm heals fast enough that I can till the land by May. I'd need to talk to someone first, though. With Mr. Baumgartner arrested, I might make the trip to Galveston sometime to talk to the Feed and Seed owner who would know more about the most profitable crops."

"That's a good idea. And something you can do with a bum arm."

Carsten smirked. "You're funny. That's one of the things I like about you, actually."

"Aww, thanks."

"Would you want to go see the creek skirting my property?"

"Yes, please. I didn't know you had a creek at all."

Carsten clicked to Stardust, and they moved forward, with Luella and her mount keeping pace. "When Pa got this land, he and the owner across the creek made a deal to share the water. Legally, our property only goes to the middle of the creek."

"That was nice of the man."

"So far, we've never had trouble with him. I rarely see him, actually."

"He's a hermit?"

"Not exactly, just not very social."

"I can be that way sometimes," Luella said. "I didn't really want to go to church Sunday. I was afraid everyone would treat me the way they've treated you."

"I didn't see any shunning. Was there?"

"No. I almost wish there was."

They reached the creek, and Carsten dismounted. "Why?" He helped Luella down.

"Then you wouldn't be alone. But then I noticed that people actually started talking to you this time."

Carsten grinned. "It was a nice change. I think being part of catching the counterfeiters helped. And for you, the fact that you were never part of it was an asset to you."

"I suppose." Luella walked to the edge of the creek. "This water is so clear. Are there any fish in it?"

Carsten looked down. "I don't know. I've never seen any, but I can't say I've looked long or hard either."

They watched the creek trickle past for a while.

"There's something else I've been thinking about for the future," Carsten said. "Us."

Luella looked at him, her forehead wrinkling. "What about us?"

"We've been good friends for years. I talked to your ma, and she said I could ask you." He knelt in front of Luella. "Can I come calling?"

Luella's confusion turned into a grin. "Yes."

Relief flooded him. Life had gone from the worst possible to the best in only a few days.

Epilogue

Late April 1870

Carsten had managed to keep up with the weeds with his friends' help. But now the alfalfa was ready to harvest, and he knew his shoulder would not handle that well. His friends would help if he asked them, but they had done so much for him already. It would take longer, but he would figure out how to do it all on his own.

Carsten gathered everything he needed for harvesting and tried to give himself an encouraging talk to start. It didn't work.

Instead, he picked up his scythe and went to the edge of a field. Carsten tried to hold it with one hand, but it was too much. There was no way he could swing it effectively. And his shoulder would kill him if he tried to harvest the alfalfa alone.

"Carsten!" a familiar voice shouted. "What do you think you're doing?"

He looked around to see Amos jogging toward him. He waited for Amos to come closer before speaking. "Trying to harvest my alfalfa."

Amos grinned. "I might be able to help with that." He took the scythe from Carsten. "We did it."

Carsten furrowed his eyebrows. "Did what?"

"Proved you innocent. And now everyone knows it, too." Amos turned and whistled. "Edmund, bring them back here!"

A stream of people came around the house.

"What's this?" Carsten asked.

"We're here to harvest your alfalfa for you," one of the men said.

A woman approached carrying a bag. "And we brought some food and material. The material is to make some quilts for the jail. We heard something about your desire for better bedding for the prisoners."

Carsten straightened, his mouth open, unable to speak.

Another man carrying a scythe stepped up. "We've been unfair to you. We need to make up for that."

All the tension Carsten had had before disappeared, and his words finally made their way out. "Thank you. Let's get you started. The ladies can go to the house to work with Ma on the food and quilts."

The ladies disappeared with the younger children.

"The men with scythes can start cutting down the alfalfa. Everyone else can follow far behind and work on spreading the crops out to dry. Since we have plenty of workers, I would do two spreaders to each scythe man."

The group separated into trios, and Carsten watched as they got to work. He couldn't believe this was happening. For the last five years, no one had been nice to him in this town, and now half the men were here harvesting for him. The last month had been one of the hardest of his life, but things seemed to be getting better.

Carsten knew it wouldn't stay that way forever and there would be plenty of trials in the future, but for now, life was just about perfect.

The day went by faster than he expected it would. With so many people helping, they finished shortly after lunch.

Obadiah came up to him. "The alfalfa looks excellent this year."

"Only by the grace of God," Carsten replied. "It looked pitiful just a couple months ago."

Obadiah clasped his shoulder. "I'd like to buy all of this alfalfa. Let me know when it's dry enough, and I'll bring some of my men over to bale it."

"That isn't necessary…"

Obadiah raised an eyebrow. "Your shoulder will not be healed enough even in two weeks to do the baling. It is necessary and also my pleasure. We're done with the branding and in a lull. My men need a little hard work to do for once."

Carsten grinned. "Yes, sir. I'll let you know. And we'll be sure to have a feast for them to eat afterwards."

"Your ma will be okay with that?"

"She loves feeding hordes of people."

Obadiah guffawed and went out to join the other men in the fields.

By the time the men finished, the ladies had food ready to eat. Everyone milled around the yard and sat wherever they wanted to.

"It's wonderful, isn't it?" Ma asked as she put her arm on his good shoulder.

"It is."

"You should go get some food before it's gone."

"I'll wait for everyone else. They did the hardest work."

"I'm happy for you, Carsten. You learned a lot during this trial, and you are finally getting the respect you deserve."

Carsten grinned and gave Ma a hug. "Thanks, Ma. For always believing in me."

He headed to the end of the line for food. After filling his plate, he stood there looking over everything and everyone, peace filling his heart.

Trust. He had finally earned their trust. And it felt good to trust God.

Historical Note

There were quite a few things I had to research for this book. Counterfeiting, Texas Rangers, alfalfa growing, farming in Southeastern Texas, and more. Most of it was fairly easy, but the counterfeiting and Texas Rangers were a little more challenging.

First of all, there is no evidence that counterfeiting happened in 1870s in Texas or that any of the men I made up were in fact involved. But I do know that counterfeit money has been made since at least the Roman days if not longer so it isn't too far fetched of an idea.

The other fun tidbit I researched was the Texas Rangers. Who, after the Civil War, changed their name temporarily to the State Police. However, many people still called them the Texas Rangers, so I decided to keep the name since it is more widely recognized than State Police.

Note from the Author

Dear reader,

Thank you for reading this book. Although I wrote it for others to read, trusting God is something that I still have to deal with in my own life. Everyone has hard trials to go through to continue growing in their faith in God. That includes me, and I put pieces of my own journey in here as well.

My prayer is that if you are going through a trial in your life, this book encourages you to reach out to God and lean on Him.

If you liked this book, please review it on your favorite retailer, onGoodreads, and on social media (be sure to tag me @faithblumauthor on Instagram and @faithblumauthoress on Facebook).

If you want to stay updated on my writing projects, family, and next books, subscribe to my newsletter!

Lastly, do you like getting free books and prizes and helping to promote new books? Join my street team!

Faith Blum

Special Thanks

Writing up this section is always the hardest to do. Not because of my lack of thankfulness but rather because I never want to forget someone. If I forgot to mention you, I apologize ahead of time.

This is my first published book that I brought through all the stages in the Author Conservatory, and that process was amazing! This book is so much stronger than the other ones I have published before, and that's in large part due to all the input from Kara Swanson Matsumoto, Joanne Bischof DeWitt, and Katie Philipps. Thank you so much, ladies!

Thank you so much to my beta-readers Lori, David, Joshua, Lydia W., Gail, and Naomi! Your comments and input were so helpful in figuring out where I needed to focus my edits the most.

My wonderful edit and design team: Thank you so much to Andrea and Kelsey for your edits and Catherine and Hannah for your formatting and cover design! You made my book shine extra bright.

And last, but definitely not least, thank you to God for Your motivation and inspiration for this story. I would be remiss not to thank my family for their support during some tight editing deadlines and encouragement through the entire process.

About the Author

Faith Blum is a wife, mom, author, and entrepreneur. She's published over 30 books, most of them in the Christian Historical Fiction genre. She loves stories because they can teach history, but in a fun way. It is also her way to have a creative outlet while taking care of a household and toddler.

She's been a proud small-town resident her whole life and wouldn't have it any other way. She lives in Central Wisconsin with her husband, son, and cat, Smokey. She's blessed to write as a part-time career. You can find her books on most eBook retailers.

When not writing, you can find her cooking from scratch, reading, figuring out social media content, or spending time with her family. She also loves playing piano for church and being part of the Author Conservatory.